DAYLIGHT COME

ALSO BY DIANA McCAULAY

Dog-Heart
Huracan
Gone to Drift
White Liver Gal

DIANA McCAULAY

DAYLIGHT COME

PEEPAL TREE

First published in Great Britain in 2020
Peepal Tree Press Ltd
17 King's Avenue
Leeds LS6 1QS
England

ISBN13: 9781845234706

Supported using public funding by
ARTS COUNCIL
ENGLAND

Their work will be shown for what it is, because the Day will bring it to light. It will be revealed with fire and the fire will test the quality of each person's work.
1 Corinthians 3: 13

"… the dark ages would arrive within one generation of the light – close enough to touch, and share stories, and blame."
The Uninhabitable Earth, David Wells Wallace

Daylight come and mi waan go home, Day-O
(The Banana Boat song), by Irving Burgie

To Adam, Tim, Nick and Brooke
whose children will face this kind of world
unless…
And to Michael Schwartz (1947-2018)
I miss you, Mike

FLIGHT

2084

CHAPTER 1 - BANA CITY

"Did you sleep? Tell me you slept." Bibi was at the bedroom door. The light that crept under doors and through cracks in walls and windows had gone and it was night. Sorrel shook her head, impatient with the question, which began most nights. You couldn't light-proof a house no matter what you did. You couldn't light-proof a world. Bibi came into the bedroom and sat on the end of her bed. She touched her daughter's shaven head, just beginning to grow out. Sorrel pulled away.

"I don't know how to help you." Bibi's voice shook. "You *have* to sleep."

"I can't. I've told you," Sorrel snapped.

"Pills tomorrow, then. The green ones."

"I don't want them. They make me feel *dooley*, like I'm asleep when I'm supposed to be awake, which is the whole problem, right?"

"What about that tea we tried?"

"Grammy's bush tea? I don't remember it helping. Just leave me alone, Bibi."

"You'll get sick if you don't sleep."

Sorrel met her mother's eyes. "I want to sleep *now*."

"It's time for school." Bibi held out her hand. "Get up. It's dark and you have to eat."

Sorrel ignored the outstretched hand, but she rose to her feet. She was almost her mother's height now.

"Your hair needs the razor," Bibi said.

"Razor's dull." She ran her hand over her head. She liked her hair to feel prickly, like it was alive and pushing outwards, even if it was dirty most of the time.

Her best friend, Sesame, had told her that old-time white

11

people had washed their thin hair *every day,* but nobody had hair like that anymore on Bajacu. You could be arrested for having the kind of stubble Bibi was pointing out. You would certainly be judged antisocial and have your water ration reduced.

"Get up, One," her mother said again as she left the room. Bibi refused to be called Mum or Mom or Mother; they were comrades in arms, she said – a term Sorrel had liked when she was younger, when her mother's nickname for her was Little One. As she grew older, Bibi shortened it to One.

Sorrel shook off her thoughts. Now that night had fallen, at least they could open a window. At least this house had a window.

The house on Buttercup Avenue was the most comfortable house she could remember. They had moved often when Sorrel was a child, always looking for a place in shadow, away from the sea, rivers or ravines, preferably a house angled to catch the fluky breezes that sometimes rolled off the foothills. Bibi had a knack for assessing the comfort of an empty house. Sometimes people paid her in skynuts to do it. This house had a roof of a slightly slanted concrete slab, the law after the hurricane season of '63 – an easy law to enforce, because after two Category Fives hit the island that year, there were no houses with other kinds of roofs left standing. The miners had sent their machines into the hills and dug down the white limestone. They scooped up the sand from rivers, and the cement factories ran day and night. The houses built after '63 had underground cisterns to catch rainwater, though virtually useless now. The best houses had a solid impermeable membrane on the slab roof, complicated drainage systems, a ledge to hold in the turflife, and succulents planted from end to end. The houses looked like cartoon characters with square faces, blank eyes and thorny hair; Sorrel liked the intricate shapes of the succulents and the way they needed no care. Up on the roofs, these plants either lived or died. A thick bank of succulents could lower the temperature in a house by one degree. To stop people stealing them, you had to apply for a permit to own a ladder. Very few were granted.

Sorrel went into the kitchen and opened one of the makeshift shutters. Bibi had replaced the original glass windows. The house gave a little gasp, as if pressure had built up inside during the day.

She waited to feel cooler air on her face, but nothing was moving outside. She gazed out, hoping to see the moon or stars, but it was too cloudy. There were always thin clouds now, which was good, because without them there would be no rain, ever, and the rays of the sun would be even more deadly, but she still sometimes wished she could see a clear sky. She fastened the window half open. If only she could sleep. Everybody else slept in the day – what was wrong with her?

Her mother sat at the kitchen table, her shoulders slumped. Sorrel saw the small hump on her spine that indicated her age, and she felt a flutter of fear in her chest.

Although Bibi had only been a child at the time of the Convergence, all the mid-century anger at the people who had ignored the signs of the coming crisis were directed – even now – at anyone over forty. Sorrel's Grammy had been beaten in the street more than once simply because she was of that time. People always need someone to blame, Grammy had said, blood trickling down her jawline.

"Stop daydreaming," Bibi said, holding out a cup of aloe tea and a bar of alganola. Sorrel loathed the bars, convinced you could taste the jellyfish in them. She joined Bibi at the table and booted up their PlAK.

"Don't get crumbs on the keyboard," Bibi said, rising to her feet. "See you later, One. Try to nap at breaktime."

Sorrel grunted, avoiding her mother's tired eyes and the furrow between her eyebrows. They were lucky; her mother had an in-person job at the tech centre, fixing the few old-time computers left. She was jealous of her mother's contact with people. It was that job that had gifted them the PlAK, by far their most valuable possession, with its access to websites, chat rooms and satellite feeds.

Today was payday. Maybe Bibi would be paid in skynuts. They were better than foodcards and were a good source of protein. The skynut trees had been brought to Bajacu by some long extinct migratory bird, and they had flourished, while every other type of tree thinned out and died.

She rubbed her eyes. She had a Math test today. She had turned fourteen two days ago and had made herself a birthday promise:

one day, she would find a place where it was possible to sleep in the dark and go outside all day when it was light.

CHAPTER 2 – BANA CITY

At 0400 hours, school finished. Sorrel rose and stretched. Her legs felt numb and the house closed in around her. Her mother would be back from work in an hour. She checked the water tank in the corner of the kitchen – about halfway down. Two more nights before water was delivered. Their house had a cistern from the old days, but the water truck's pipe couldn't reach it. The tank filter was dirty, and she should clean it, but it was hard to clean anything without using precious water. She replaced the cover. Maybe tomorrow. At least school was over and she could go online and talk to Sesame.

"A Tribal girl was captured by the Domins. Last week. She was scavenging near the mountains near where the Toplanders live," Sesame wrote, the words coming up like bubbles on the PlAK's screen.

"Everyone scavenges," tapped Sorrel, using a string of emojis to show her disdain. "She could have been any Bana girl!"

"It was how she was dressed. Strong. Muscles in her legs. I heard she fought off the Domins like a feral; killed one and ran. No Lowlander could do that. They caught her, though."

"You're just bored."

"Yeah. Aren't you?"

Yes, Sorrel thought, *I'm bored*, but she was tired of Sesame's stories and signed off, sending SEW to her friend, their code for Sudden Ending Warning. She would sit outside for the remaining hour of darkness.

She opened the kitchen door and walked onto the hard dirt, which her grandmother had called "the garden" until the day she died. The light from the kitchen fell into the yard. She sat in her favourite spot on a large, smooth rock in the shadow of the house.

15

Her Grammy had once told her why the rock was there – their house on Buttercup Avenue was on the Sabana Plain, laid down in geologic time by the Ama River, which had brought the big rocks with it. You could still see them around Bana – some had been coated white long ago and still had flecks of paint in their grooves and indentations. The Ama River had broken its banks the year of the Category Fives and killed an uncounted number of people who had been living too close. Now the sea was even nearer to the Ama River and soon there could be a huge body of brackish water cutting right through the city. Too much water and too little water, at the same time. Lowlanders were always thirsty.

But outside in the dark, she couldn't stop hearing Sesame's story-teller voice.

"They call themselves Toplanders," she had said. "Rich people who went up to the mountains. After the tunnels in Bana collapsed."

"Ridiculous," Sorrel had scoffed.

They were still able to visit each other then, although they could travel only at dawn or dusk. They would often lie head to head on the cool tile floor at Sesame's house, arms outstretched, pretending to be starfish.

"The hurricanes would have killed them, Ses. What would they eat?"

"I read they grow food."

"What kind of crops would survive the rain bombs, the dust storms? It's foolishness."

"Rich people can do a lot."

"They can't do miracles. And what about the ferals? They don't have them in the mountains?"

"I didn't see anything about ferals."

"These are just stories. What d'you have to eat?"

"Usual."

"I'm so sick of alganola."

"Yeh, me too. It's why I like to think about people living in the mountains growing food."

"Why didn't other people join them up there, then? No way that could be kept secret from the Domins."

"There are others up there too – different to the Toplanders. They're like the Tainos – that's what I heard."

"The who?"

"Tainos! You were never any good at history. They're the people who lived here before everybody else. Tribals, they're called now."

"*Guata*, Ses, you should definitely be a writer." They giggled at the forbidden curse word and their outstretched fingers touched.

"I think the rich people just left and there are no tribals," Sorrel said. "They would have died in the heat or the storms, or the ferals got them, or they starved to death."

"People always find a way. I heard the Toplanders are in that old army camp. You've seen it on SATMAP."

"Foolishness. The Domins would definitely find them if they were at Cibao camp."

"They have slaves. All women. And there's a terrible man up there."

"Just stop, Ses. Monster stories."

She had not seen Sesame in person for more than a year and she missed her, if not her fantasies.

Now she heard the noise of working people going home after a night of work, some on foot, some on skateboards. She liked to watch the young workers who had enough balance and strength to skateboard. She could hear them jumping over the cracks and buckled asphalt in the road and she thought of the Tribal girl that Sesame told her about, fighting like a feral, running, then still being caught.

Could there be people, maybe even young people, living together in the mountains, outside Domin control? There were caves in the mountains, so shelter was possible, and there were simple ways to condense water – every school child had to do basic survival training. But what was there to eat in the mountains? Would it really be so much cooler? What would they take with them? What path would they follow? Every night they would have to find somewhere shaded. This was all foolishness. That Tribal girl. The Domins would have staked her out on the Burning Rock Plain – no witnesses, no questions asked – and left her there to sizzle up and die. The whole idea of the mountains

17

was too dangerous. She turned her thoughts to Bibi's return and what they might eat. The rock she sat on still held some of the day's heat.

She loved rocks. Her clearest childhood memory was of a shallow hole she had scraped out under a rock when she'd been about six, living somewhere else. She had been able to crawl inside the hole and lie on her side, knees to chest, the rock almost touching her shoulders. The darkness under the boulder was different from the night outside. The earth had cradled her, and the rock had been like a low sky.

Once, she had dared to go to it in the day. She had dressed in her oldest clothes and, though feeling guilty, had climbed into the bath and soaked herself. She did not remember anything about getting there except the lacerating light. Her clothes began to dry immediately. In her scramble to crawl out, her cheek had brushed the rock's rough surface and she'd cried out and jerked away. When her mother saw the blister, Sorrel had confessed that she had been outside and Bibi had confined her to her room with just alganola and water, no PlAK. She still had that scar.

The sky was lightening in the east and the air seemed to contract, like the singeing of her skin against the red-hot rock so many years ago. Sorrel felt short of breath. A sheen of sweat spread over her exposed skin. She wanted to shed her clothes. Once the sun was in the sky, human sweat would dry between one breath and the next. Skin would crack like the salt flats near the Burning Rock Plain. People without efficient sweat glands never lived past childhood.

Where was her mother? Bibi was never late. Maybe she had gone to the seawall for provisions: dried and salted jellyfish, alga-oil for the bars that were their main source of food; maybe some of the mussels which now clung to every surface in the sea and smelled faintly of paint.

Sorrel hoped for a sea-egg. They carpeted the seafloor but were too deep for a casual wader and were harvested by licensed divers. There was a black market, of course, and her mother knew all the sellers. She wished for a fresh one, still smelling of the sea. They would crack it and fry it, add salt, and eat it at the kitchen table.

The sound of skateboards had stopped. The footsteps she

could hear sounded too rapid. People out there were running. No one ran anymore; it wasted energy. She thought again of the Tribal girl running, being caught and dying on the Burning Rock Plain. Sorrel walked to the gate and looked down the road.

People were travelling through the gloom in groups: men and women carrying children. A few old people. Some hauled small carts; others were laden with overstuffed backpacks. She heard the clip clop of a mule or horse – a rare sound. Those people out there had very little time before the sun came up and they would face dawn danger.

Bibi had told her once that there had been dawn bunkers in case you were trapped outside at sunrise, but they had been built in the wrong places and the rising sea had claimed them.

"Sorrel!" It was her mother's voice. She strained to separate Bibi from the groups of hurrying people. "Why're you outside?"

"I came to look for you. You're late. What's happening? Why's everyone on the move?" She could see her mother's face now, drawn with worry, glistening with sweat. The half-moon circles under her eyes were deeper and fear flashed in her eyes.

"Inside," Bibi said, looking over her shoulder.

"Those people are going to be caught outside."

"Maybe," Bibi answered. "Maybe. They *might* find an empty house."

Sorrel noticed her mother's weariness and pushed away the anger that lived high in her chest. "Let's eat, Bibi. Then you can go to bed."

"There's no time," Bibi said. "We have to get ready."

"Ready for what?"

"Inside," Bibi said again.

The heat had settled over the house. They sat at the small kitchen table, breathing shallowly.

"We're ordered to leave," Bibi said. "They say this hurricane season will bring a storm surge along Buttercup Avenue. They're posting the evacuation orders tonight."

"Good," Sorrel said, surprising herself.

"*Good*?" Bibi pointed at the open window and raised her voice. "You want to struggle to find a new place? To have to *fight* for it, maybe?"

"Did you hear anything about the Domins catching a Tribal girl? In the last day or two?"

"What?"

"A Tribal girl. Someone who lives – lived – in the mountains?"

"There are always stories like that, One."

"They could be true."

She faced her mother. *We're so weak*, Sorrel thought. *She's so weak*. "You have Level 3 access. Are there Tribals in the mountains?"

"You know I can't talk about that."

"You'd say no, if it wasn't true. Bibi, I want to leave Bana. I want to find other people. Young people like me. I don't want to spend my *life* with you in this dead city."

Bibi reached out a hand to her. Sorrel ignored it. "I know this is hard for you –"

"Hard? It's *impossible*. I don't want to live like…like a bat or an owl or a worm. We're all just circling around." Sorrel took a deep breath and stood. The heat was making her dizzy. "You don't have to come," she shouted. "You go look for another house. You keep going to work until they think you're too old and then they'll cut your water ration, they'll take back the PlAK; maybe even your foodcards will be stopped. One day you'll go outside to find food and the Squad will get you. Or the ferals. Or you won't make it back before the sun comes up and you'll roast like a pig on an old-time barbecue and the good people of Bana will walk past your corpse. Remember that body we saw before the shaving law, that day at the waterfront? Remember how the cartmen threw her on the sea? And how she crumbled and floated away like ashes?"

"Why're you bringing that up?"

"Because as long as we stay here, that's what's coming for us!"

Bibi went over to the bucket in the corner and took out the rag. She slopped the scummy water on her face and neck and then held it out to her daughter. Sorrel took it.

"You're forty-five, Bibi; I'm fourteen. Maybe there *are* Tribals in the mountains and we can join them."

"Even if there are, the Domins will arrest us before we've gone five kilometres. Or the ferals…" Her mother's voice trailed off and silence fell between them. The rag was warm in Sorrel's hand. Already it was nearly dry.

"What about your father?" Bibi said, avoiding Sorrel's eyes.

"What about him? He's in prison."

"I've been to see him. Maybe you can go one day."

"He's never getting out. You need to face that."

You can't trade off my life for his, she wanted to say but swallowed the words.

Silence fell between them. "Look what I brought." Bibi said, reaching into her bag. She held a sea-egg with clipped spines. "You get the frying pan. After we eat, we'll sleep. When it's dark, we'll talk some more and decide what to do. I can't think in the day."

"I wanted an egg," Sorrel said, softly.

"You always want an egg."

CHAPTER 3 – BANA CITY

She turned on the PlAK. It was 1100 hours and her mother still slept. Sorrel had only managed a restless two hours. She dressed in a sports bra and shorts, but didn't clean her teeth, because she wanted to keep the taste of the sea-egg in her mouth. The daytime heat was still not at its height. People used to think that they couldn't bear it any hotter, until they found they could.

She looked for Sesame on Neurality but her friend was not online. Once she and her mother left Buttercup Avenue that night, Sorrel knew she would probably never see her again or even speak to her. They would never see her father, either.

She went to the collage of unconnected and unverifiable information held by surviving websites and servers which could crash at any moment. An alert about breached seafloor cables flashed up. There had been new arrests of people who had tried to tap into the cables.

Bibi had Level 3 information clearance, because it was her job to make sure machines accessed only the permitted level of the owner. Sorrel had hacked into her mother's portal a year ago which could have got them both arrested. Only Sesame knew just what level Sorrel could access. It was safer that Bibi didn't know.

Although she regarded the historical websites as no more than a collection of myths to distract everyone from the present, she loved to read them and always started there when she browsed: clear water in rivers and streams, stored in reservoirs then sent to kitchens and bathroom through pipes. No limits on how much a person could use. Meat eaten every day; pigs and chickens raised in buildings, eggs a boring breakfast food. Felines and canines were "pets" living with their owners. It was at least a year since Sorrel had last eaten a starving baby feline, caught by her mother on the way home from work. Parks and museums and churches; films and plays and concerts. Cars everywhere, people flying in airplanes – airplanes! – to visit family abroad. It was even harder to imagine that people used to fly to their island to lie under the sun on a sandy strip of land they called a beach.

And the hair sites: women with hair that fell to their chins, their shoulders, even to their waists – hair long enough to make into all manner of designs: plaits and corn rows and bumps and locks and weaves and buns and French braids; hair that women washed every week, not once, but twice each time, using conditioners and potions, which had to be rinsed out with *drinkable* water. Sorrel loved the styles called Afros, which were like halos – when hair was part of a woman's beauty.

She'd wonder which countries were the luckiest, out there, behind their closed borders. Was it easier in the places with winter? Some were icebound most of the year and could grow no food, but they had more water. Was it better to be inland? Here there was the relentless swell of the sea, ever closer, ever higher.

Heat radiated off the walls and she pulled the desk to the centre of the room. Time to get down to business. She logged into Level 3 and went to SATMAP to get a bird's eye view of the island, knowing the images were between four and six months old. Only Level 1 would guarantee a realtime view. She was sure she could break into that, but it was too dangerous to try while they were still under Domin surveillance in the city. But still, there was the encroaching sea, the battered Sabana Plain on the south shore, the mountains rising to the north. She could see the roofs of the old hotels and the tower at Caicu Airport, now half underwater, with large mats of seaweed clustered around its sides. That kind of seaweed was toxic. Every year a few starving people were seduced by the easy harvest and died, their fingers, toes and lips turning black.

She moved her fingers over the screen up to the mountains, following the traces of an old road towards what used to be the army camp of Cibao, until it stopped in front of a wall behind which, Sesame said, the rich Toplanders lived.

She leaned back in her chair. If they were going to leave Bana, they had no choice but to go to the mountains. Find a good cave.

Maybe they would be able to grow some types of food, even find fruit on trees. And sleep at night.

She started searching for old tracks and paths. The roads would be patrolled by the Domins, using drones or ATVs.

She saw the scars of earthquakes, numerous mudslides and rock falls and vertical cliffs. She zoomed in to a curving line of rocks – some small, some giant-sized, flanked by trees. The trees were bigger near to the rocks. It had to be a dry stream bed. She traced it down to the foothills where it disappeared. Could they find that place from Bana?

"Sorrel?" Bibi came out of her room. "Child, you have to sleep."

"I'm not a child," she retorted. "Look at this. It's an old stream bed. See the line of the rocks?"

Bibi approached and peered over her shoulder. "Could've been a stream. So what? There won't be any water now."

"We need to go to the mountains."

"But –"

Sorrel slammed the PlAK shut and burst into tears. Bibi reached out to hug her. Sorrel pushed her away and walked over to the sink. Her head pounded and she was ashamed of crying.

"We have to t-try something," she stammered. "What do we have to lose?"

"Pretty much everything," Bibi said. "Like my job, which gives us food. We could be dead within hours of leaving Bana. We could starve. Die of thirst. Be torn apart by ferals. And the Domins…"

"You're just afraid to try *anything*."

"At least we know what *this* life is like."

"And it's *guatan* awful."

"Don't swear."

Bibi walked over to window, now shut tight against the day. She rested her hands against the shutters, wincing a little at the heat from the wood. Then she turned to face her daughter. "I *want* to give you a chance of a better life, but what if this is all there is? Surely if it was better in the mountains everyone would be there?"

"Not if everyone is afraid to try. Can't we at least think about it?"

"If we wait too long, all the good places in Bana will be taken."

"I'm not staying, Bibi. I'm going."

"Sorrel…"

"No. I'm done. Are you going to help me find a way out or not?"

"You're all I have, One. Let's look together, then."

Sorrel reopened the PlAK and they sat in front of it. "We need to find a landmark.'

"For what?"

"For where the stream bed ends," Sorrel said pointing with the cursor.

CHAPTER 4 – BIBI

They called it different things: Change, then Crisis, followed by Emergency. Then they changed it to Disruption, then Disaster. In the end, it didn't matter. Finally, they – you never knew who "they" were – realised that the worsening climate converged with poverty, geography and history. So now they call it the Convergence.

I was eleven and lived with my parents in the foothills overlooking Bana. Higher elevations were cooler, so we were luckier than others and I believed we deserved it. Every night my mother and father watched good-looking men and women on television report on melting ice, swirling snowstorms, cities swallowed by earthquakes. We saw people washed away by rivers that broke their banks, taking villages with them. We watched whole islands drown.

All this was far away. I thought the news was boring and had nothing to do with us. The decapitated mountains were not ours, nor were the children swept away by raging water.

I remember the sizzling morning I went to Rae Wharf with my mother and saw the fishers leaning against the rum shop, the women facing them with empty baskets, their faces slick with sweat.

"No more fish," the men said. "But we have a few sea-eggs."

My mother responded that we were not *that* desperate.

Not long after, the crops began failing and the fruit trees stopped bearing. We tried to grow some things in our garden, but they all died. I remember this one pumpkin vine which produced a flower and then a pumpkin. My parents watched it as if they were tending a sick child, then one morning it was gone. Someone too hungry to wait, my father said. After that, the vine withered and died.

The water supply failed in Bana and I went with my father to the Ama River, which still had pools of water. Thousands of people lined its crumbling banks carrying containers. Rich people put pumps in the pools and sucked them dry into tanks in the back of their trucks. I remember we had to walk a long way to find a pool that was not stirred up. I don't remember the journey back to our car with my water bucket full, but it must have been difficult.

I went to campus school until I was fifteen. I was good at tech support. Halfway through my final year, the power supply could no longer support air conditioning. I never went back.

I remember the cars strewn around Bana after the roads melted, until a storm lifted them and cast them in the sea. They stopped giving hurricanes human names the year of the Cat Fives – that storm was Theta 24. We became trapped in cycles of flood and drought. The pandemic of 2020 had already shut down country borders, but the viruses had found their animal hosts and they sickened us in waves. The animals we let loose to roam and graze the almost barren land mostly starved and died, then shrivelled into ash. A few horses and mules survived and did not become feral. The pigs and dogs that survived banded together in feral packs and began to hunt and feed on us. We tried poison and traps, but they bred too fast.

Then it became too hot to go outside in the day; the dust storms started and the sun began to blind and kill. Our neighbour, Neema, was the first I knew to die – a quiet soft-spoken woman made cantankerous by thirst and hunger. She tried to scratch out her husband's eyes and he threw her out. All we heard was the bang of the front door and then her screams. No one opened their doors to her. I did not ask my parents why.

I still think of my father and the way he died. He was out all night at the seawall foraging for food. Daylight caught him there. He tried to get into one of the dawn bunkers, which still existed then. The people inside would not open the door. They shouted to him that there was no more room. I never saw his body and I don't know how the Domins, who brought the news, knew who he was, because there was nothing left. All they gave my mother was his wedding ring. For a long time, I thought about his bones.

I didn't believe the sun could destroy bones, at least not so quickly, and I imagined the gold ring, loose around a finger bone, against the blackened dust. I also thought about the food he might have found, which we did not get. I wondered who would have taken the food and left his ring.

I didn't witness what the sun could do to people until after Sorrel was born. I was always sorry she saw it, too.

Now, my headstrong daughter, my only child, wants to abandon the safety of the dark. I tell her Tribals don't exist – they are a myth that the young have created to hang onto hope – but the Toplanders are real. I've seen classified reports about the Toplanders and their raids on young Lowlander females to use as slaves. The raiders are led by a cruel, reckless man the reports call The Colonel. There was Essan, a girl Sorrel's age, who disappeared while she was out searching for food and we knew it was the Domins who'd caught and sold her to the Toplanders. And Amaryllis, snatched from her doorstep in the presence of her parents and never heard from again.

What I know for sure is that in this time of killing heat and hunger, there is no safety anywhere. Every day the sun comes up it will blind or kill us if there is not a roof over our heads. Every day the Domins are on the hunt for young women and the ferals can surround us and tear us apart.

I'm forty-five and the end is coming fast for me. What use am I without my daughter? Maybe the only thing I can give her is a chance to escape this hell. To die with her would be better than to die alone.

Two days had passed, and the loudspeakers had begun transmitting evacuation orders, throughout the night. The stream of people on the road had disappeared and Sorrel knew all the best places in Bana would already be taken.

On the SATMAP, they had found traces of an old aqueduct close to the dry stream bed, which they could use as the point to start their journey to the mountains. They'd searched for possible hiding places along the way: big rocks, caves, old-time trees, but knew the images they were looking at were old.

Her mother was sleeping. It was not yet peak heat. The street outside was silent. Were they the only ones left without shelter in Bana? The shutters were closed against the day. Sorrel wanted to be moving, to be distracted from the risks of their decision, to face whatever was ahead.

She began to make a pile of the things they would take with them: solar charger, graphene filter, a funnel, neemoil. All the alganola they had. A tube of algafuel. Four sky nuts in an algaskin. A change of clothes. Three pairs of socks. Dark glasses. UV proof hat – all of them, life or death choices. She considered an almost full tube of old sunscreen and put it down. No amount of sunscreen would help if they got caught outside in the day.

She started to search the house for portable items they could trade along the way. She made a separate pile: a second, broken solar charger, an algaskin of bootleg rum, which, on consideration, she rejected because of its weight. Another algaskin full of sugar – sugarcane had survived the Convergence and grew in roofless buildings. Sorrel pulled everything out of a cupboard until she found an old tarpaulin. She cut it in half for use as groundsheets.

"Pack the sunscreen," Bibi said, coming out of the bedroom, rubbing her eyes.

"Why? Are you going to give orders the whole time?"

"We might be able to go outside in the mountains because it's cooler, but there'll still be UV rays to think about. Maybe there'll be trees, but we'll still be in danger from dappling. Pack it."

"It's toxic."

"Toxicity takes years."

Sorrel shrugged and added the sunscreen to the pile. Two sporks. Two cups.

"What's that pile for?"

"Things to trade," Sorrel said.

"We need to carry as little as possible. We'll have the PlAK, if it comes to that."

"I'm not giving up the PlAK." She glanced at her mother – the skin loosening at her neck and hands, her face freckled and marked by sun damage from before the Convergence. Bibi had told her that then some people lived past eighty because of good food, eight hours of sleep most nights and antibiotics. *Maybe I should leave her,* she thought. *Maybe I'd have a better chance on my own.*

You and me against the world, her mother used to say.

When do we attack? Sorrel would reply and they would laugh. They hadn't played that game in ages.

Their eyes met. Bibi's looked weepy and sore. "I'll be fine," she said. "You're only fourteen. You can't go alone."

Sorrel shrugged. "The old aqueduct comes out right by Guaqua. That's a two-hour walk from here. Do we need a weapon?"

"We need a knife for digging and reaping whatever we find to eat. Two would be better. Wrap the sharpest ones we have."

Maybe the knife would be needed for something else. Sorrel tried to imagine killing someone who stood in their way. Stabbing them. Feeling the knife go in, warm blood on her hand, hearing their screams. Man or woman? Would they leave the body outside for the ferals? Could she kill another person?

She was nine when the Domins had kicked down their front door and taken her father. It had been at dusk, just as Sorrel was waking. Her mother was in the bathroom.

"Don't come out, B! Hide, Sorrel!" her father had shouted.

She had crawled under her bed and heard the beating, her father's grunts and cries, trailing off into silence. The Domins had taken him away by the time they emerged from hiding and she was left to imagine what the beating had done to his body. A crumpled piece of paper lay on the kitchen table. Bibi had read it out loud, tears sliding down her cheeks. "The whole skynut tree?" she whispered. "Not a first offence?" It was a stupid, despairing act – to cut down the tree with nuts still on it.

A year later, Sorrel had watched from a window as two males killed an old woman on the street. As with her father's arrest, it was dusk, and she had just got out of bed. She'd opened a window and saw an old woman carrying a basket of old-time custard apples, probably on her way to one of the illegal, pop-up markets. No one liked old people; they ate, got sick, didn't work and were burdens on the young. Besides, they were the cause of the Convergence. It was not exactly legal to kill them, but even at ten, she knew people looked the other way. The two young males on the other side of the road were wearing the Squad badge of violence trainees. People avoided violence-trained men, but the old woman did not notice them until they began to cross the road. She looked around, searching for help or escape, and then stood still. Laughing, the males took her basket away. The taller man slapped her, as if he were conducting an experiment. When she fell, the other man kicked her once, twice. The old woman folded her arms over her head, offering no resistance. "We should rape her," the taller man said, biting into a custard apple.

"What for? She's dried up like dead coral." They took up rocks from the side of the road, and took turns smashing her head until it wasn't hard anymore. They wiped their hands on the old woman's clothes and walked away, eating the custard apples.

A few minutes later, she heard the howls of feral canines and shut the window. In the morning, the old woman's body was gone. She never told anyone what she had seen.

"You're daydreaming again," Bibi said, staring at the PlAK. "Pack some string. And rope. Wrap it around your waist. How many knives do we have?"

"One good one. And an old paring knife but it's dull."

"Pack them anyway. Come, look at this – looks like an old

water tank. Before the climb gets really steep. About a third of the way up."

"So what?"

"Means there used to be water there. Maybe it's where the dry stream will take us. Maybe it's shelter. Come here. Your eyes are better than mine – what's this?"

Sorrel stared at the PlAK. "I don't see anything."

"Those poles – what are they?"

"Tree trunks?"

"Way too straight."

Sorrel suppressed her irritation and went back to her packing.

"Whoa!" Bibi said. "They're cable-car towers!"

"What?"

"It's an old cable-car line! Just what we need."

"What's a cable car?"

"Machines that took people to high places in the mountains, places too steep for roads. Carriages that ran on, well, cables. Ski resorts used to have them."

Sorrel wanted to ask what a ski resort was but there was no time for stories. She couldn't visualize a cable car and didn't understand her mother's enthusiasm for a few poles in the ground.

"I didn't know there was ever a cable car on Bajacu," Bibi said. "Must have been from the tourism years. But don't you see, One? This is what we've been looking for – it's like a signposted trail, taking us up the mountain. Look how high it goes. All we have to do is find that water tank." Bibi shut the PlAK and hugged her daughter. Sorrel did not remind her mother that there was every chance that nothing the PlAK showed them still existed.

At 1300 hours they began to eat everything they couldn't carry. They pulled the bucket of water into the middle of the living room and wet themselves every half hour. They drank as much water as they could. They ate slowly, sipping at the air between bites, as if that too was food. The heat reached its height and plateaued. They tried not to move.

At 1400 hours, Sorrel logged on to Neurality from Level 4 and looked for Sesame, but her friend was not online. *I hope you're right about the Tribals, Ses, and wrong about the Toplanders.* Especially the part about the female slaves. She stared at her own profile picture, now at least two years old. She had the same straight eyebrows as her mother, the same amber eyes, the same slightly triangular ears – elvish ears, her father used to say, tracing them with his finger.

"What are elvish ears?" she'd asked.

"From books I used to love. It's not important."

At 1600 hours they showered. They stood back to back and turned the pipes on full, using nearly all the aloe vera soap to scrub their bodies. The water was almost too hot to bear but they stood under the shower anyway and let it run down their limbs. It felt reckless. Decadent.

At 1700 hours they used the electric razor on their own bodies, then on each other for the parts they couldn't reach easily. Sorrel ran the razor over the slight swell of muscle in her mother's thighs and was relieved. Muscle meant strength. But it all felt too intimate.

"Should we take this with us?" She asked Bibi, holding out the razor.

"How heavy is it?"

"Not too heavy."

"Then yes. At least we can do our heads. Best not to stand out too much."

At 1800 hours, the cracks of light in the house began to fade. They slathered their skins with aloe and neemoil. They filled their backpacks, dressed and drank some more, then slung full water algaskins across their bodies.

"They're going to bump around and be annoying," Bibi said. "Let's see if we can strap them tighter." Her mother fashioned straps for the water bottle and settled hers between her breasts. "That's better," she said. "Can hardly feel it there. You want to try?"

Sorrel practised walking; felt the bounce of the bottle on her hip. "No, I think this is fine." Her small breasts were not capable of nestling anything. Maybe they would never nestle anything.

They left the house at 1900 hours and joined the handful of people still in search of shelters outside the Immersion Zone. It was strange to be with other people. Under a streetlight, Sorrel caught the eyes of a boy about her age hurrying in the opposite direction. He raised his hand at her. She ducked her head and didn't return his gesture. She knew very little about boys. Sesame had a brother, Bracken, whom she had met a few times, back when they visited each other's houses. He was close to nineteen then, sombre and mute. He had a deformed arm and had not been hormone-assessed at puberty by the Domins and had escaped violence training. Some of the females in her education cohort had lost their brothers to the Squad and talked about them in chat rooms. They found it hard to believe their brothers could become so dangerous, but Sorrel remembered the males who had killed the old woman and eaten her fruit, so she remained silent. For some boys, violence training didn't take, and they were sent back to their families, but they were ashamed and often walked out from their homes when the sun was at its height and were never seen again.

Tribal. What did it mean? Was a Tribe something you belonged to, filled with people who had your back? The old-time meaning of the word suggested being from a particular place and connected to it over generations, but if there were Tribals now, surely, they would be from different parts of the island? Did Tribal mean a group of families, connected by blood? Was Tribal the opposite to civilized? It was easy to be drawn to a fable of groups living outside, in harmony with each other. She was going to miss Sesame's stories, even if they turned out to be myths to make people feel better about their reality or to keep them in line. She hooked her thumbs into her backpack straps and leaned into the weight of all her remaining possessions. Despite the water she had drunk, she was thirsty again and they were still on Buttercup Avenue.

CHAPTER 6 – GUAQUA

They followed the main east-west highway across Bana to Guaqua, once marking the end of an old-time tramcar line, once a market village, once a university town. Bana's main roads still had streetlights and their yellow glow fell onto the ground in triangles. Guaqua was a hodgepodge of broken buildings along the ridge of the Ama River valley, outside the Immersion Zone. A few people walked the lanes and streets, looking for any kind of place with a roof. No one spoke; everyone held their destination close. The evacuation announcements had stopped.

"Did this town have a square?" Sorrel whispered to Bibi, trying to make sense of the mounds of rubble and shattered sidewalks.

"Yes, kind of. Not really a square. But after one of the rain bombs, the Domins piled up all the wreckage in the middle. Over there." Bibi nodded at a dark, irregular mountain of debris, more in shadow than light. "The river used to be behind those buildings, way down. I went there once… when it was a river."

The streetlights revealed the roofless, windowless buildings, but the slope behind them was in total darkness and that was where they had to go.

Bibi went behind a crumbling wall between two buildings and pulled out the PlAK. They had to be sparing with its use until they could use the solar charger. "There was a message from Sesame," she said, "but read it when we stop. Look. I think the aqueduct is down there." She pointed. The cracked road was edged by slabs of sidewalk, uplifted and moved sideways.

"I can't see anything. Can you? Can we really get down there?" Sorrel asked.

"We'll have to. Look, there's a house over there with some light inside. Maybe we can see better over there." Further up the road,

Sorrel saw light flickering through windows in a standing wall. "No roof," she said. "You can't call that a house."

"People are inside, though."

They walked closer and Sorrel heard low voices. A child cried and a woman's voice shushed and sang an old lullaby. Maybe they were resting, but it was unlikely – travellers had to use every hour of the night to search. How could they survive without a roof? The shadows thrown by the walls would move around – would the people have to stand or lie in them, hiding from the sun?

Her mother touched her arm. "Come on."

They scrambled around the side of the house and stood at the top of the black slope. Bibi shone the small PlAK light at the immense darkness of the river valley.

"Use the searchlight function," Sorrel said.

Bibi shook her head. "Uses too much power."

They saw no sign of a track leading down the hill. Perhaps no one else had thought of the old aqueduct as a trail to anywhere. Sorrel squatted. The soil was sandy and loose and she could see rocks and a few very small cacti close by, too small to reap, even if they had the space to carry them.

"It's an abyss," Sorrel said.

"We go down sideways," Bibi replied. Her boots slipped but she caught her balance.

"Maybe we should go back," Sorrel said "There's time. We'll find a place tomorrow night."

"No," Bibi said. "We've decided. We've made a plan. You hold the PlAK; your balance is probably better than mine."

They slipped and slid down the slope led by the PlAK's small light, directed at their feet to avoid turning an ankle. They could not look ahead. They did not know where the hill ended or if they were going in the right direction. Sorrel felt her thighs stiffening from the movement of walking downhill and she wondered how her mother was doing. Bibi was ahead testing each foothold before transferring her weight. It was good not to be alone in the darkness. They heard their own scraping, tentative steps, and the fall of loose stones. At least there were no more mosquitoes on the Lowlands, but maybe they had survived in the mountains and if they had, there would be fevers.

Her breath was now coming hard. Sorrel looked up at the sky, searching for any signs of the coming dawn. Bibi stopped. The night was impenetrable – not the velvet black of old-time night skies, salted with stars – she had only seen pictures of those – but the dark grey of dust from those far-off places that had lost all their water. What would happen to them if there was a dust storm?

"Come on," Bibi said, as if she had not been the one to stop. The incline had become less steep. Sorrel turned on the PlAK searchlight to sweep the landscape and her mother did not object. Rocks everywhere. What chance was there they would stumble upon the aqueduct in the darkness? Maybe this was the last night of her life. Would dying of heatstroke hurt? Would it burn like the searing rock on her cheek? Might have been better to be caught in the frozen parts of the world. Freezing seemed less painful than burning. Stupid thoughts. Here was where they were.

All they could see of the land was shape and shadow, the hard, smooth silhouettes of rocks, the spiky, irregular outline of stunted plants.

"Turn off the searchlight," Bibi said.

The land was flatter now. They began walking faster. A giant rock loomed to their left. "Let's rest for a bit over there," Bibi said, pointing. "Have a little drink."

"Do we have time?"

"We can't just blunder around until it's day."

Sorrel felt chastised and a small moment of gladness at her mother's company evaporated. Bibi led the way to the rock which loomed above their heads. It was nestled into the slope on one side; jutting out smooth and round like something man-made. "What's holding the rock in place?" Bibi said. "Why didn't it get washed away?"

"Who cares? It's big, that's probably why."

"Not too big for a rain bomb. There must be some kind of obstacle." Bibi's voice trailed off as she ran her fingers along the rock. "Bring the PlAK over here."

Sorrel shrugged her backpack off and the loss of its weight made her feel light. She joined her mother and in the PlAK's light, they saw there was a gap behind the rock.

"See? Nothing's holding it." Sorrel said. "Let's go."

"But feel here – at the back. It hasn't been smoothed by water."

"So what?"

"Everything that could be shelter matters," Bibi said.

Sorrel looked at the clock on the PlAK – minutes to midnight. They had been walking for close to four hours and had not yet found the aqueduct. "We need to –"

"Shhh! What's that noise?" Bibi hissed.

"I don't hear –"

"Climb! Now!" Bibi yelled.

"What?" Sorrel heard a low, rumbling growl, coming from behind them.

"*Guata,* Sorrel!" her mother cursed. "Climb when I tell you!" Sorrel hesitated and her mother grabbed her hand, pulling her towards the gap in the rock. She looked over her shoulder and saw something low, racing out of the dark. Feral.

"You go first!" Sorrel cried, as they squeezed into the narrow space behind the rock. She stuffed the PlAK inside her clothes. Bibi didn't argue. She found footholds and climbed.

"Hurry!" Sorrel panted. Her legs were exposed; she heard a snarl, then scrabbling at the base of the rock and the feral's teeth closed on her right boot. She kicked. If she lost her boot, they were dead.

Something bounced against the rock. She heard the animal yip and her boot was free. She began to climb. She saw her mother's extended hand but ignored it. "Did it bite you? Are you bleeding?" Bibi demanded.

"I don't think so. It had my boot. *Guata.* I left my backpack in the open. Everything is in it." She realised Bibi's pack was also gone. "You threw your pack at it?"

"Yes. There was nothing else."

"We've lost everything on the first night? Except the PlAK and a little water."

"We need to fight it off. Let's wait for a bit."

They sat, back to back, knees to chest. The feral snuffled and barked below. "It's going to get into the packs while we're waiting," Sorrel said. "If it gets the rest of our water and food, we'll die."

"I know, but the packs are sturdy. Let's think. Is it only one canine? Ferals aren't usually alone."

"One bit my boot, that's all I know."

They waited, listening, and watching the sky for signs of lightening. Sorrel's fear ebbed. If the choice was between frying on the rock and being torn apart by ferals, she knew which she'd choose. People used to be burned at the stake, she remembered from the history module. Maybe their nerves shut down and apart from the first scorching, they felt nothing after that. She offered her mother a drink from her algaskin and had a sip herself. Her breathing slowed and she looked around at the landscape slowly revealing itself. Rocks and sand and shadow. One backpack, not far from them, still intact. No sign of the feral.

"I think it's gone," Bibi said. "We've lost a lot of time. We should find the backpacks and see if we can shelter here."

"Here where?"

"I think there might be space behind this rock."

"It's way too small. Maybe we should go back up the hill and see if those people we saw in the roofless house will let us stay with them?"

"What, retrace all our steps? And that house had no roof."

They were silent. Sorrel looked again at the sky, but all she could see was a grey swathe of dust. She stood. "I'll go down."

"No, I'll go."

"I'm stronger. Faster. Just wait."

"Listen to me, One. Please."

"No."

Sorrel inched her way over the back of the rock. When she stood on the ground, she felt around the space that Bibi had pointed out behind the rock with her hand. Definitely not enough room for two. She turned and scanned the expanse of rocky earth ahead; her mother's backpack was quite close. It was torn, but the contents were safe. *One down*, she thought.

She didn't want to leave the rock. She was sure the feral was waiting them out. They had survived because of their willingness to band together with other species. People had reported seeing bovines, porcines, canines and felines, hunting and scavenging together, forgetting old relationships of predator and prey. They rooted for food in garbage dumps, hunted the hordes of rats that populated the emptying lowland towns, and waited where rivers used to flow for whatever was washed down by rain bombs. She wondered what they drank during the long dry periods between rainfall.

We need to be like them, Sorrel thought. *Cunning and ruthless. Opportunistic.* She stepped out of the crevice, ready to retreat, her mind on the knife in their backpacks.

The grey-black night was turning to the white-grey of dawn danger. She saw the feral, a canine, about three metres away, lying against a small rock. She couldn't estimate how big it was. It lifted its head and growled, baring its teeth and gums.

She tried to reach the nearest backpack with her foot, but it was just out of reach. She looked up again. Not long before sunrise.

She stepped back into the crevice and leaned against the hill, assessing how much shadow they could share. There was no time to dig a tunnel. She thought of teeth ripping skin. How much damage could one feral do against two humans without weapons? Suppose there was more than one? She wanted to feel rage instead of fear.

"Look at what's holding the rock in place!" Bibi shouted from above. Sorrel swore under her breath and with her hand, traced the line of the rock until it met the dirt. A small shower of soil dislodged itself, and she could feel a shallow hole. She dug with her fingers and touched something hard. She peered at it, bringing her face close. "There's a tree root," she called to Bibi. "There must've been a tree here once and the rock washed up against it." She traced the shape of the root with her fingers. It was massive.

Sorrel started to scrape away the dirt.

"What're you doing now?" Bibi called.

"I don't know. But the soil feels so loose, maybe there's –"

The dusty soil cascaded around her feet as she began to follow the roots of the tree with her fingers. They went up, up, and made an arch above her head, connecting with the rock. If they dug some more…

"Come down, Bibi! You were right. Maybe we can fit – come help me!"

Her mother slid down almost knocking Sorrel into the open.

"Can you dig?" Sorrel said. "I could try and reach the closest backpack. Maybe find the knife inside."

"Be careful." Bibi began scraping away dirt with her hands.

It was getting lighter. Sorrel felt breathless. The canine saw her and rose to its feet, growling. It began slinking towards her, back arched, head low. One backpack could be reached with just three long strides. She took a few deep breaths, pushed down dread, and raced into the open. She scooped up the backpack and turned on her heel. She heard the scrabble of the feral's feet coming for her. Two more strides and she was behind the rock. Sweat poured off her face and she thought she would faint.

"Good job, One," Bibi said, reaching for the pack. "Go inside. Rest." She gestured at the space she had carved out under the roots of the giant old tree. "Leave the other pack out there. It'll soon lose interest. One thing about alganola, ferals don't think it's food."

Sorrel eased herself sideways into the crumbly space, her chest heaving. It was just big enough for both of them. They sat cross-legged, facing each other. She leaned her back against the earth and unwound her water bottle. "Don't drink it all," Bibi said.

"You really don't have to tell me that." Sorrel took two deep swallows.

The musty darkness of the tree root cavern settled around them. Finally, they heard the retreating footsteps of the feral. "Let's push some of the loose dirt out," Bibi said.

When they had finished, Sorrel's limbs felt heavy and she could barely keep her eyes open. Despite the danger they were in, she was suddenly sure she could sleep, even though the sun was beginning its climb into the sky. She settled her shaven head against the earth and found herself thinking about earthworms. They had all died in the Convergence, along with the reptiles. Bajacu had no lizards anymore. Ants had survived, though, and it was said there were bees in the mountains. Still, she expected to feel the squirm of some kind of life, but the soil gave up nothing. She looked up at the tree roots above her and thought they were like fingers. Her mother made a little snore and Sorrel closed her eyes.

CHAPTER 7 – BIBI

I met Drew after my father died outside the dawn bunker. My mother came to me and said we were almost out of money and the Domins were going to get rid of the old currency. She had an old friend at the tech centre and she convinced him to give me a job rebuilding obsolete electronic devices. Drew sat across from me and showed me how to build functional PlAKs out of almost nothing. I used to watch his long, nimble fingers and the spray of hair across the back of his hand as he soldered. I began to imagine those hands touching me.

We were there at night, of course, and spotlights from the roof lit our work area, leaving our faces and bodies in shadow. We were not supposed to talk, but we techs had developed a rudimentary sign language that the supervisors never noticed. I was more familiar with Drew's hands than his voice. One day he offered to walk me home at the end of our shift.

By then my mother and I lived in a small ground floor apartment in an old part of Bana. Six nights a week, Drew walked me home and we parted at the front door. He lived with an older brother; his mother had died giving birth to him during hurricane Chi 18 and his father had died of one of the new viruses two years before we met. He asked me what my dreams were and listened to my answers. I loved him for that.

We had found a bench under a tree on a patch of open land and would sit there in the dark, sometimes for as long as three hours. He kissed me and I opened my mouth to him, and I felt the world step back. He stroked my face with the hands I had begun to dream about. He smelled slightly of metal.

One day he asked me to go to his home with him – his brother having finally found work. Once a month we left our shifts early, claiming illness or emergency, took off in different directions and met at his door. His bed was unmade and narrow. It forced us to lie close. Our breaths mingled, and our skins were slick together. I loved the feel of him inside me.

Neither of us thought I was fertile – my periods were rare, and Drew, who had been tested for violence training, probably did not have enough hormones. We figured we were safe. I did not ever want to bring a child into this chaos. I was just shy of twenty-eight when I woke in the middle of the day and vomited. My mother brought me a double ration of water and I could see the worry in her eyes. "Who is he?" she said.

"I met him at the tech centre. His name is Drew."

"Bring him here."

"To live?"

"Yes. Why not?"

"He has a brother."

"Bring the brother too."

We found a bigger place; half of a house on the way out of Bana. We called it the Halfway House. Drew's brother didn't come to live with us, but he sometimes visited Drew at the tech centre and they would talk during break.

My belly grew. I was both starving and repulsed by the thought of food. I was also terrified. If the Domins learned I was a fertile female, if I birthed a boy with the right hormone levels, they would take the child and I would be given to a Domin man.

I was lucky; I had a small belly and no one at the tech centre noticed what I carried under my white coat.

Drew had a friend with a doctor uncle, and we went a few times to speak with him. He told me what to expect and said he would help when it was time for the baby to be born.

My daughter was born on the kitchen table of the Halfway House just as the sun came up. I always figured that's why she couldn't go to sleep at sunrise. A daylight come baby, my mother said, as she handed her to me.

Sorrel woke, washed in sweat and disoriented, surprised to have slept at all. She was cramped and stiff but didn't want to wake Bibi by moving. It was lighter in the tree cavern and she looked at the intricacies of the root system that sheltered them. What kind of tree had it been? A big one, perhaps centuries old? Were the roots living or dead? If dead, why had they not decayed? Maybe the soil was too sterile. A ray of sunshine touched the ground at her feet, and she assessed its angle. Had to be past midday. The hottest time. The silence of the day lay over the charred land.

Her stomach felt hollow and she was desperate to move. She wanted food. She wanted more than alganola. She remembered her Grammy's stories about the time before the Convergence, how people got on airplanes to fly to other countries and the food they ate. "We used to complain about how the food was awful," she had said.

"What kind of food?" Sorrel had asked.

"By the time I flew, there was no more food. But my mother used to talk about it – food on little trays. Drinks too. Things like wine and whisky."

"How many times did you fly?"

"Only once. To New York. Before they closed the borders. Before the Renaming."

Grammy had told this story dozens of times, but every time a new detail was revealed. The tall buildings in New York. Air conditioning and heating. Restaurants. People selling food from wagons and stalls in the street. Flowering trees. Parks with green grass. People outside in the day, rushing to their jobs and families, jogging with earphones. "We thought there was no going back, ever," Grammy always said at the end. "We thought everything would get better and better forever."

"What d'you miss most?" Sorrel said.

"Patties," her grandmother said.

Bibi stirred beside her. Sorrel saw the glint of her mother's eyes. "You slept?" she said.

"Some. I'm stiff."

"Me too. It'll take me an hour to unwind. Hungry too. Let's eat something. Drink a little too. Find the knife. You have better eyes – has the feral left? We need to know if there's only one."

Sorrel squinted at the land outside. The sun could blind you. There was the canine, lying in the narrow shadow cast by a rock. It had returned or perhaps it hadn't left. A porc snuffled at the sandy soil in the blazing sun.

"At least one canine and one porc," she said. "How've they survived outside?"

"Small. Fast. Good at finding shelter. Eat anything."

"Why didn't the Domins hunt them before there were so many? We could've eaten them."

Bibi shrugged. "They tried back in the day. They bred fast. Hid well. Some were killed and eaten, but then people got sick. I don't know."

"I hope they didn't get into the other pack."

"We should drink. Look for the big knife."

The water was warm and thick and failed to quench Sorrel's thirst. She rooted in the backpack and found some alganola and the kitchen knife. "A little luck," she said, giving it to her mother.

The ray of sunshine softened and retreated. Eventually, twilight settled around them and they breathed more easily.

"We don't have much time before it'll be full dark," Bibi said. She groaned as she tried to move her limbs.

"We can't stay here through another day. We need the other backpack."

"I know. How big are these ferals?"

Sorrel shrugged. "Compared to what? Can you stand?"

"I think so, but we should think about what we're going to do."

"You and your plans. Give me the knife."

"The canine will go for your throat," Bibi said.

Sorrel stood outside the root shelter, her back to the giant boulder, knife in hand. She could just see the shapes of the two ferals, their heads turned away. She tried to judge the distance – ten, maybe fifteen metres.

"Come out," she whispered to Bibi.

"You go right," Bibi said. "I'll go left. I'll take this pack – you'll be able to lift the other one more quickly. Then we run."

Sorrel spotted the second backpack just as the canine's head turned in her direction. She could no longer see the porc. The feral raced towards her, closing the distance in seconds. It skidded to a stop just outside of kicking range and snarled. Its yellow teeth were ringed with black and she thought of carrion. Then it jumped for her throat and she felt its hot breath on her face. She sidestepped and lashed out with her knife. It circled, low to the ground, growling. She kicked and it dodged her foot easily. It leaped for her chest while she was off balance and she slashed out again, disgusted by its stinking, rotten breath. Her knife sliced the canine's neck and it yelped. She stumbled and fell, rolling away from it as fast as she could. Where was the porc? How badly had she cut the animal?

She jumped to her feet and looked around. No sign of the canine. There was a trail of blood through the sand, leading into the rocks. She had fought off a feral and she yelled in triumph. Then she heard sounds of struggle somewhere behind her and ran in the direction of the root-shelter.

Bibi's back was against the big rock. A small porc was standing in front of her, swinging its tusks. Sorrel kicked at the animal with all her strength. It swung around to face her, lowered its head and charged. She screamed and sliced at it; kept slicing until the knife went in through muscle to bone. The porc squealed and fell, pulling the knife out of her hand.

"Make sure it's dead," Bibi panted. "What happened to the canine?"

"I cut it and it ran off." She went over to the porc. Its eyes were open and glassy, and it looked well fed. She wrinkled her nose at its smell and pulled her knife free.

They stood together, hands on their knees, their breathing harsh. Sorrel wanted to howl at the sky.

"That's a lot of food," Bibi said, nodding in the direction of the dead porc. "We should have learned how to hunt them. Pity we have to leave it." She met her daughter's eyes. "You keep the knife," she said.

"You go first," Sorrel said to her mother.

CHAPTER 9 – THE WATER TANK

The skies were clearer that night and the dim moonlight made it easier to see. The stream bed became more obvious the farther they walked, and just before daybreak, they found the water tank Bibi had seen on the PlAK at their kitchen table in Bana.

"That's where we can hide today," Bibi panted.

"It's open to the sky," Sorrel objected. She'd never thought the water tank a useful destination – given that the stream bed was dry.

"Yes, but maybe like those people we saw in the roofless house in Guaqua, we can move around to avoid the sun. Maybe there's even some water inside. Or some plants."

The concrete water tank was cool to the touch. "But how're we going to get into it?" Sorrel asked.

Bibi collapsed on a patch of gravel. "I can't go any further, One, I can't. We have to find a way to get inside that tank."

Sorrel stared at her mother. This was only their second night. "Lie down, Bibi. Drink a little. We're going to be fine."

Sorrel got the PlAK out of her backpack and kept its light on the water tank as she circled it. The top was uneven and breaking away. There were a few holes in the side, some quite low down which meant the tank could only hold a little water. A rusted pipe curved over the top edge but the rest of it was missing. As the sky lightened, she noticed the bushes were bigger and different in the hills, and she thought the tank might almost – almost – be in shade when the sun came up. There were a few vines as well. She could just curl her fingers over the edge at full stretch of her arms, but she doubted she had the strength to pull herself up. Her thoughts whirled. She looked around for rocks. There were many but they were either too small, or too big to move, even with Bibi's help.

She pulled herself up to where the land had built up around the tank, then launched herself at the rim. Her fingers held her for a few seconds then she fell back. She tried again, kicking with her feet to give her momentum, but it wasn't enough.

Bibi joined her and they stood side by side. "You okay?" Sorrel said, staring at the distance to the top of the tank.

"I know how we can do this," her mother said and there was excitement in her voice. "I'll kneel down. You step onto my back and then you can easily climb in."

"Then what, Bibi? You'll be on the outside, I'll be on the inside."

"I'll hide."

Sorrel shook her head.

"One, listen to me. I've had my life. Let me do this. Please. We do have some rope. If we both get in, we can pull up the backpacks too. It's worth a try. There's no time to argue about it."

The growing heat lay down upon them. Sorrel dug for the rope in her pack and left it on the ground. Her mother knelt as close to the old tank as possible. "Step on my shoulders," she said. "Not my waist."

"I'll take off my boots. If I get in, throw them up."

"Good idea." Her mother knelt.

Sorrel looked at the back of her mother's neck. Everyone was thin now, but Bibi was way too thin. She placed her palms on the tank to steady herself and stepped onto her mother's back, expecting her to collapse. "Quickly," Bibi grunted. Sorrel got her arms over the edge of the tank and kicked with her legs, her feet scrabbling for footholds. Her right foot found something sharp and she pushed against it. Then she had her waist over the edge, and she could see silt piled up on one side and a small pool of water on the other – almost as if the tank had tipped and been righted in an earthquake or landslide. A piece of an old metal slab, probably a part of the tank cover, leaned against the side. She scissored her legs over the edge and dropped into the silt. It was degrees cooler inside.

"Send up my boots and the packs," she cried. "It's cool in here. I can get you up!" She hauled the metal slab to the side with the silt and made a ramp of sorts.

Bibi threw up the rope and it landed in the tank. Her mother had tied a rectangular rock to the end. Sorrel pulled up both packs and her boots and untied them. "Stand where the rope comes over!" she shouted, then made her way to the top of the slab, hoping it would not slide down into the silt. When her head emerged from the tank's shadow, she felt the rolling heat of the day approaching. "Make a sling," she called. "Put it under both arms. Then climb."

There was a broken pipe to one side, and she looped the rope around it, pulling as her mother created slack. She heard Bibi's frantic breathing and then the top of her head emerged. A blade of sunlight sliced down, a metre away from the tank. The rope went slack suddenly and for a moment, Sorrel thought her mother had fallen back, but then they were facing each other, the wall of the tank between them. Sorrel reached under her mother's arms and pulled. Bibi hung on the edge for a moment and Sorrel felt the makeshift ramp shift under her feet. She pulled again, staring into her mother's eyes. They fell together into the old water tank just as the sun found them.

CHAPTER 10 – ON THE RUN FROM THE DAY

The strangest thing about being inside the water tank was how light it was. It was day and there was no cover. Sorrel could not remember ever being able to look up in the morning. She knew the sun rose in the east but had never seen a sunrise. She risked an upward glance at the sky and was surprised to see it was pale orange. "Put on your dark glasses," Bibi said. She had not moved from where she had fallen after their struggle to get in.

"It depends where the sun is when it gets overhead," Bibi said, reading her thoughts. "We might be lucky. The hill above us might give enough shade."

The tank had a silty floor. The scummy water in one corner was about 15 centimetres deep and smelled of rot. Sorrel stripped down to underwear. She dipped her rag into the water and wiped her bare limbs. "Must have rained here not long ago. D'you think we can drink it?"

"Maybe. We do have the filter. But we don't have an empty container."

"We should've thought of that."

Her mother shrugged. "We didn't have much time. Let's eat and drink. One of us will have to watch the shadows to make sure we move with them. The other must sleep."

They ate. "Tell me about things you used to eat before," Sorrel said. It was a game they had played when she was much younger.

"When we're settled, I'll tell stories all you want. But now we just have to get through this. You sleep first."

Sorrel laid out her ground sheet on the rough silt. It was more comfortable than the bed she'd left in Bana. She let her feet touch the side of the tank, hoping that if it started to heat up, she would feel it. Bibi sat cross-legged with her back against the tank. She looked exhausted.

"I should've peed before we got in here," Sorrel said.

Her mother nodded at the water. "Might as well, if we can't drink it."

"I'll try to hold it." Sorrel had never spent this long outside, never walked this far, never slept without a roof over her head. Maybe they could stay here forever, a life stripped down to nothing at all. But they would need food and water. And other people. Her last thoughts were of Sesame – she had not read her friend's last message. Maybe she and her family were now at the bottom of the Immersion Zone.

It was afternoon before her mother woke her. "You let me sleep too long!" Sorrel said.

"You were sleeping at last. You didn't even flinch when I wet you down."

"It's passed 1200 hours. The sun didn't come in?"

"No," Bibi said. "The rays came about halfway down the tank, but we were still in shade. We've been lucky."

"You sleep now," Sorrel said. She dipped her scarf into the puddle and wondered how far down the concrete floor was. The silt in the water was slimy, which meant tiny plants grew in it, which meant it had been there for a while. Why hadn't it evaporated? Maybe the old stream still ran, but underground?

That would be worth finding out.

She thought about a river, a real river, with cold, fresh, clean water flowing over stones, making deep, blue pools and Immersion Zones which brought a choice of exile from the city, or death by drowning.

What had this place been like before the Convergence? There would have been big trees, streams, a bridge, a road, which cars would have driven on, going up into the hills, to do what? What had been the purpose of the water tank? She sat, leaning against the tank, and tried to figure it out. The stream had flowed from mountains to plain, joining other streams and tributaries, making a bigger river, on its way to the sea. People had built the tank to store water from the stream, but then what? The severed pipe must have taken the water somewhere, to houses, to the old reservoir, perhaps. She had read about the reservoir that used to serve Bana before the desalination plant was built. It had broken away in the rain bomb of '67 and wiped out a string of settlements of several hundred people. There were no reservoirs anymore – nothing could stand up to the force of the rain bombs – when an entire year's worth of rain could fall in a few days. She was beginning to feel like a ghost. She ran her hands over her head – they would soon need to take out the razor. Sorrel wished she had thought to pack a mirror. In their rush to get into the water tank they had not left the charger outside in the sun so the PlAK hadn't been recharged. There was nothing to do but sit and wait for nightfall.

It was dusk before her mother opened her eyes. "Time to be on our way," she said. Sorrel found herself reluctant to leave. The tank felt safe – cooler than ambient and safe from ferals. She climbed onto the old cover and peered out, flinching from the glare of the retreating sun. When had the blaze of sunsets she knew only from the Literature module ceased? When had daylight started to end in this ominous, slow erasure?

"Come," Bibi said. "Untie the rope and stow it. Look around, make sure we're not leaving anything. You go first."

"So what are we going to do? Follow the stream bed like we planned? Or look for the cable car line?"

"The columns," Bibi said. "Steeper but more direct."

"Direct to where?"

"To high up. Remember we saw them on the PlAK?" Her mother seemed rested and stronger. "Don't climb with the backpack. Give me yours and I'll send them both over."

Sorrel pulled herself over the edge of the tank and dropped to the ground. She almost twisted her ankle and thought how easily this journey could end in disaster. "Send the packs," she called, hoping she would be able to get herself out of the tank. It took a few tries, but Bibi made it.

Using the weak light of the PlAK, they searched for the metal columns that they'd seen. The searchlight caught the first column and they walked over to it. "Can you see the next one without the light?" Bibi said.

Sorrel narrowed her eyes and looked. "Yes, just."

"Turn off the PlAK then. It needs charging. Let's go."

Sorrel counted in her head as they passed the columns. She wished she knew how many were ahead. She wished she knew exactly where they were going. How would they find other people? Perhaps once they were high enough and found a good place to stay, they could look around for the signs of others. What would a good place look like? Caves had advantages but could collapse in earthquakes and could easily be turned into a trap by ferals. Maybe this was a reckless and doomed journey. Maybe moving was all that was left to people. Her sore hands burned, and her muscles ached. She leaned against the straps of her pack and plodded upwards in the darkness.

The time between towers grew longer, although they were evenly spaced. Sorrel realised they must have slowed down. She wished she could see what was behind them to assess how high they were, but it was too dark.

Two hours into the climb, Bibi sat heavily on a rock.

"Rest, Bibi," Sorrel said. "I'll look around for a place to shelter. I don't know if we can walk the whole night. It's too steep. Drink some water. Rest. I'll soon be back."

They were on a hillside. The unfamiliar plants were mostly shoulder height and crowded together in places. Perhaps they could lie where the plants were densest and that would provide enough shade. The vegetation was definitely thicker and different from on the Lowlands. There were still succulents, but there were many other plants; some could even be called young trees. Perhaps they had fruit or nuts or leaves which they could eat.

Something straight ahead in the bush caught the pale light of the moon and Sorrel felt a pulse of dread. Ferals? She didn't think so; the reflected shine had the stillness of metal. She pushed her way through the underbrush and saw what she assumed was an old cable car. "Bibi!" she yelled. "Over here!"

The car was slightly tilted against a large rock. She threw her weight against it to see if it was stable, and it held firm. The windows and doors were all closed. There was lettering on the side and she traced it with her fingers, but she couldn't make out what it said. The door handle was stuck fast. She doubted if she had the strength to shatter one of the thick glass windows.

She walked around the side of the car closest to the slope of the hill and saw a makeshift ladder, leading onto the roof of the car. They were not the first to find this place and maybe there were already others inside.

"A cable car," Bibi said from behind her.

"Yeah, but look. Someone's used it, maybe is still using it." Sorrel kicked at the side of the car.

"You'll hurt yourself," Bibi said. "Let's listen."

"Listen for what?"

Bibi put her palms on the car and pressed her ear to its side. "I don't hear anything."

Sorrel was sick of caution. She climbed the flimsy ladder, ignoring her mother's pleas to be careful. There was a roof hatch and she tried to pry it open with her fingers. It was heavy, but she persevered and finally got it up. She lowered herself inside.

The inside of the cable car was dark. She felt around, barking her shins on metal – presumably the old seats. She ran her hands over them, and something flaked away – rust? Paint? Rust was a hopeful sign – it meant moisture. Perhaps even rain. She called to Bibi to set up the PlAK and charger and to bring one backpack at a time.

The interior of the car was revealed by the dawn: forward-facing seats, only the metal left, dusty floor with human footprints, blackened glass windows. A door at the rear. The door was locked from the inside with a latch. If they could open it, that would let out some of the hot air when the car heated up. The only place to lie was on the floor between the seats.

"Should we stay here, though?" Bibi said. "What about those footprints? Maybe the bushes outside would be, I dunno, less risky. Suppose whoever made those prints comes back?"

"Don't we want to find people? Are we going to assume everyone we encounter means to hurt us?"

Bibi sighed. "We need to find the right kind of people. We need to control how we meet them, maybe watch them for a bit. Assess how strong they are. We need to avoid being surprised. These footprints could belong to anyone – Toplanders, Squaddies. Others we've never heard of."

"Or Tribals who would take us in."

Sorrel sat in the dust. "Someone's been here but not all that recently. See, the edges of the prints are blurred. I think it's worth staying here for a night. There's no shelter that's without some risk, Bibi. At least we'd be safe from ferals – they'd easily get us if we were under bushes."

"One night," Bibi said. "And we take it in turns to sleep."

CHAPTER 11 — THE CABLE CAR

They ate their alganola bars and drank the warm water from their algaskins. They sat in adjacent aisles, their backs against the car, legs outstretched. The dust on the floor was thin; there was no softness to this shelter. Sorrel erased the human footprints in the dust with her foot.

"Now they'll know someone's been here," Bibi said.

Sorrel didn't answer. She was sure she would not be able to sleep.

Bibi met her eyes. "Dawn used to be hopeful," she said. "Maybe you went to bed with a problem, maybe you had bad dreams but when you woke up, the light made you feel hopeful. I had my best sleep just before dawn. Now we're on the run from the day."

"Not just the day," Sorrel said. Then she smiled. "Grammy used to say 'darkest before dawn'."

"Birds used to sing. It was called the dawn chorus." Bibi hummed a tune Sorrel had never heard.

"What's that?"

"Old folk song. *Daylight come, and me waan go home*," her mother sang. "It was about banana pickers."

"You sleep first," Sorrel said. "I don't think I can."

Her mother's expression was unreadable. "If anyone or anything is gonna attack, it'll be soon. Before it's too hot." Bibi said.

"I know."

Bibi lay down in the dust and closed her eyes.

They remained in the cable car throughout the third day. Sorrel let her mother sleep. She wished they had the use of the PlAK, but the battery was almost dead; they'd arrived too late to set-up the charger. She wanted to check her messages – what was happening in Bana? Had those who remained in the Lowlands drowned? Was there anyone left as witness?

At about 1500 hours, Sorrel heard scratching sounds. Peak heat had passed. She touched her mother's foot with hers and placed a finger on her lips. Bibi's eyes opened. "D'you hear that?" Sorrel whispered.

Bibi cocked her head. "Wind," she said. "The bushes against the car."

"I think it's an avian."

"If it is, it's dangerous. And there won't be just one. They travel in flocks."

Then they heard a sound like gravel thrown against the roof by a giant hand. "Rain!" Bibi said.

Sorrel shot to her feet. "I'm going outside," she said. "Right now!"

"No, wait –"

Sorrel ignored her mother's warning and climbed out under a low grey sky. Big drops of water splashed onto leaves and soil, making small pools, which disappeared in seconds.

"What're you doing?" Bibi shouted from inside the car. "Come back inside!"

"I'm staying!"

"If it really rains and we leave the hatch open, the car will fill up and we'll drown. Come inside!"

Sorrel heard the worry in her mother's voice, but if she was to drown, she wanted it to be a fight with rocks and water, a battle with the elements. She didn't want to drown inside a closed space. She could face broken bones but not a fight for air. "You come up," she shouted to her mother. "Take the PlAK – put it away and stow the packs off the ground. Bring the algaskins."

"Suppose it's a rain bomb?" her mother cried. "The cable car will be washed away with all our stuff!"

"If it's a rain bomb, we'll be washed away long before the car." Sorrel jumped off the roof, collected the PlAK and charger and handed it to her mother inside the cable car. "I'm staying outside. Pass the algaskins and the funnel, then shut the hatch."

She stood outside with the algaskins and funnel at her feet. The big drops became more frequent and closer together. She turned her face upwards and closed her eyes, letting them hit her in the face, welcoming the slight sting. Then she heard a slashing, hissing sound and the drops became a deluge. Real rain. Drenching rain. Rain that could make waterfalls. She stood with her head back, eyes closed, mouth open. The water tasted sharp. It streamed off the hill in muddy channels, circling the cable car, digging at her feet, making mud. She filled the algaskins one by one and wished they had brought more, although water was heavy to carry.

When her thirst was slaked, she pulled off her sodden boots and socks and stripped to the skin. The rain sluiced off her head and shoulders and she ran her hands over her body, feeling the dirt and sweat of their journey dissolve leaving her light and strong. She shivered a little, a feeling so unusual that she was not sure what it was at first. *She was outside in the day.* She beat her clothes against the side of the cable car and wrung them out, then she lay them on the bushes around her and surrendered to the sensations of her body.

The rain was slowing. She could feel the heat gathering again. The air itself felt wet. Her feelings of exultation vanished.

She heard the cable-car hatch open. "Are you okay?"

"More than okay. It was great."

Bibi asked nothing more.

Sorrel gathered her wet clothes in her arms. She felt a flicker of embarrassment at greeting her mother naked, then a surge of defiance. Who cared if she was naked in this shattered place?

As she approached the ladder, Sorrel saw that the rain had washed away the dirt that covered the writing on the side of the cable car – El Dorado. She climbed up the ladder.

She laid her soaked clothes on the roof, wondering briefly if they would blow off as soon as they dried. Before she climbed down into the car, she looked up at the sky. It was the clearest she had ever seen it and almost blue. The land was clean and so was she. She let herself down into the car. Her mother said nothing about her nakedness.

CHAPTER 12 – THE CULVERT

Water had leaked in through the hatch of their shelter, turning the dust inside to a thin sludge. There was a dry space at the rear because the car was tilted forward. Her mother had stored the backpacks on top of the metal seats during the storm, so they weren't soaked.

Sorrel hesitated, not wanting to lie in dust or sludge, but there was no choice. She felt briefly sorry for Bibi who had missed being in the downpour. Then lassitude filled her. She stretched out in the dust and plunged into sleep.

It was dark when her mother shook her awake. "Time to go, One," she said.

"Maybe we should stay. It's a pretty good shelter."

"We need water. And the people who've been here will be back."

They left the cable car and resumed their climb, following the columns in the light of the fully charged PlAK. The slope became steeper still and sometimes they had to drop to all fours. "The trail is getting better as we go higher," Bibi said. "That's worrying."

"I want to find people. I still don't see why we have to presume everyone is dangerous."

The greyish night of the Lowlands had given way to a deeper blackness. Her mother was falling behind again. Sorrel stopped. "Are you okay?"

"I'm just tired. Maybe we should have stayed in Bana. Found a new place, like we always did."

"We did the right thing," she said, but her certainty was ebbing.

"We'll never know that for sure," Bibi said.

Sorrel shone the light around, looking for an easier way. There were a few rocks in step formation to her right and she wondered if they had been placed there, but when she stepped on one, it rolled away. She looked for handholds, but the bushes were too thin and whippy. "Should we rope ourselves together? Maybe I could go ahead and send down a rope for you?"

"No. We should stay together."

"At least hold my belt then."

"Just climb," Bibi said.

One foot after another, thought Sorrel. They climbed. Then, as the slope became too steep, they crawled.

"I need to rest for ten minutes," Bibi said.

Sorrel swept the PlAK's light in a circle. The bush was thicker, taller, full of shadows, but there was no obvious shelter. "We can't stay here."

"I know that," Bibi snapped. "I'm asking for ten minutes, not a week."

Sorrel swallowed a retort. "I'll have a look around."

Her mother nodded. She sat with her head lowered, the curve at the back of her neck pronounced.

Sorrel struggled into much thicker bush. The PlAK revealed tangled shapes, and slopes of light and shadow. Outside the sweep of the searchlight, the blackness was total. If they found good shelter, she would research the various kinds of plants. Perhaps there were new high-protein shrubs – there had been many experiments in the early 70s. Maybe food was right here.

She tripped on something and fell hard, knocking the breath out of her. She cursed herself. Dreaming while awake could get her killed. She lay with her cheek on the ground for a moment, then stood. She shone the light in a circle, first at shoulder height, then above her head, and it fell on a cliff face with a square opening cut into it, about two metres off the ground. A culvert for water. And it looked dry. She wondered why it hadn't been filled by the recent rain.

What had tripped her up? She shone the light at her feet, and it fell on an obelisk shape. She scraped away the dirt and saw a number carved into it – 21. Below that, Miles to Kingston – Bana's old-time name before the Renaming. Then she spotted a trail leading away from the cable car columns, slightly downhill into the bush. She directed the searchlight at the plants closest to the trail – some branches were cut or bent back. Someone was keeping this trail open. People.

She looked up at the lightening sky. They had to find shelter before the sun came up. A hundred metres or so down the hill she could now see the last cable car column they'd passed on the way up. She wanted a direction. A path. Surely no one would go to the trouble of keeping a trail open if it led nowhere? And it was much flatter. She ran back towards Bibi.

"I found a trail!" she shouted. "A real trail. Come, get up, we don't have much time!"

"A trail to where?"

"I don't know. But we might as well follow it. We'll have to run."

"I can't run, One. I can't."

"Come now! Get up," She grabbed her mother's arm and pulled.

"One. I am done. I can't even shuffle, much less run."

Sorrel was caught between the approaching dawn and her exhausted mother. She remembered the square hole she'd seen in the hillside. "There's a dry culvert near the trail. It'll be cool inside. It's dry too. Wait there. You can't stay here in the open. Come on Bibi! It's hide or run now. No other choice."

They stood looking up at the culvert. "We should both stay here," Bibi said. "You don't know who made that trail or where it leads. It's reckless, One."

"We can't *live* in a culvert. We'll drown in a rain bomb, if it falls in the right place. We'll get no warning. There's no food. No water, until there's too much water. We can spend this day here, sweltering underground, but then what? Same choice tomorrow night. Might as well face it now."

"Daylight is nearly here – how far can you get?"

"I don't know, Bibi! I don't know but I want to have a look. I probably have half an hour. Look, there's no time to argue!" Sorrel cried. "*You* have to trust *me* now! Climb on my shoulders, like we did to get into the tank."

Her mother said nothing more. Sorrel knelt, Bibi stepped

between her shoulder blades, and then her weight was gone.

"You take the packs," Sorrel said, heaving the first one to the culvert's entrance. "I'll be able to run faster. The PlAK's inside this one. See if you can position the charger so it catches a little of the sun. Try to sleep."

Bibi hauled the packs in. "You have water?" Her mother's voice sounded hollow and beaten. Sorrel was sure she couldn't continue up the mountain.

"Yes. Hang in there, Bibi. I'll be back."

She left her mother and ran towards the trail. Thirty minutes more and the scorching heat of the day would bear down upon her.

CHAPTER 13 - CENOTE

Sorrel felt light without her pack and she ran faster than she thought possible, her water bottle bouncing against her hip. The trail became even flatter and made of gravel. Plants crowded the path and scratched at her arms and face. With every step, the day came closer, every breath she took was hotter. The glare made her squint and she realised her dark glasses were in her pack.

The trail curved sharply to the left and before she could stop her flight, she was tumbling; then rolling, down and down a treeless slope covered with sharp grass that came out of the ground in clumps. Then she fell through space. She hit water and sank. The water was warm and still. Her lungs were bursting, her eyes open, but she could see nothing except the killing light above. She kicked out with her legs and hit something hard and sharp. She felt it slice through her pants. She kicked again and this time she rose towards the sun. Her head broke the surface and she sucked air into her lungs, coughing and spluttering. Her boots were dragging her down. Now she would die in a pool of water somewhere in the mountains, and her mother would perish in the culvert, waiting for her.

Her foot touched the submerged object again and she pushed herself upward once more. Then something clamped her wrist and pulled her towards the surface.

She lay full length on burning pebbles; saw human feet wrapped in what seemed to be animal skins in front of her. "Get up, unless you want to die right here and now." It was a female voice. "I'm counting to ten: one – two – three…"

Sorrel got up. A girl stood in front of her, hands on her hips. She was drenched as well, and her arms and legs were wrapped in some type of gauzy material. She had a tangle of curly hair – hair! – half hidden by a woven hat. She wore no dark glasses and had fierce black eyes. *A Tribal*, Sorrel thought. *They're real.* The girl turned and strode away. Sorrel quickly came to her feet and followed her.

The girl moved swiftly through the bush, despite the heat. There was no obvious trail, yet her steps were sure and long. A machete was slung across her back. She wore a brightly coloured scarf around her neck which she'd pulled up over her nose, and gloves with the fingers cut off. Sorrel wondered where she had managed to find them.

Sorrel became breathless. The girl lengthened her lead.

"Wait!" Sorrel called after her, but she didn't look back or slow her pace. Sorrel followed her into a bamboo thicket, the trunks large and scratchy. Then she disappeared.

Sorrel stopped. It was slightly cooler in the bamboo grove. It was hard to keep her eyes open against the glare. On the Lowlands, she would have already been blinded, but the vegetation softened the blaze of the sun. She thought of her mother in the dark culvert and the possibility of a rain bomb. She turned in a circle but couldn't see the girl. Why would she have brought her here only to vanish? She called out again and heard rustling to one side.

"What the *guata* are you waiting for?" the girl demanded, pushing her way into the bamboo. "You want to die outside?"

"I didn't see where you went."

"You're *guatan* slow. Can tell you're a Lowlander. You're *guatan* lucky I saw you fall into the cenote. This way!"

Sorrel struggled through the bamboo trunks. They were as thick as a man's thigh and tore at her clothes. Then, ahead, the girl turned sideways to go through a narrow opening in a sheer cliff face. Sorrel followed her. The opening led them to a cave, and inside the darkness was total.

The girl's footsteps stopped. Sorrel took a few steps forward and bumped into her. She smelled of green things and sweat. "What're you doing?" she snapped. "Don't move. Wait for your night vision."

The air in the cave hung still and was neither hot nor cold.

Sorrel could hear and see nothing, but she sensed they were in a much larger space than the opening had suggested. "This is a cave?" she said, to break the silence.

"Of course, it's a *guatan* cave. Where else could we go?"

Very slowly, the darkness lessened, and Sorrel began to see some details. The floor of the cave was rocky and dry, scattered here and there with loose stones or pebbles. The roof was slanted to the floor, as if a slab of stone had fallen. She stretched out her hands and touched nothing.

"Are you going to kill me?"

"Kill you? You sure are a Lowlander. There's no need to kill you. All we have to do is put you out."

"We? Are there a lot of you?" *Definitely Tribals*, Sorrel thought. *Ses was right after all*.

"Nineteen. You'll see. We had a death last week, a girl, maybe about your age. How old are you?"

"Fourteen. How did she die?"

"A feral got her. An avian. Dug out her eyes before we could beat it off. After that, well, there was nothing anybody could do."

"Ferals are up here?"

"Ferals are everywhere."

"I left my mother in a culvert."

"You're in the mountains with your *mother*? Why?"

"She was tired. Couldn't walk anymore. The day was coming."

The girl snorted. "I meant, why are you with her at all? We have no need for old people."

"She's my mother. I couldn't leave her in Bana. I told her I would come back for her."

"Your choice. You know the way out."

"I could never find my way back."

"I think we can move now."

"My mother..."

"Forget your mother."

"I can't. I won't."

"Well, tell your story to Caroni. That's all I can say. She'll decide."

"Who's Caroni?"

"The Zorah."

"What's a Zorah?"

"Elder."

"How old is she?"

"Thirty-five or so. You finished talking?"

"What's your name?" Sorrel asked.

"Emrallie is my band name."

"Are you a Tribal then? We thought you were a myth."

She shrugged. "That's what Lowlanders call us. And yeah, let them think we don't exist. We go now. Stay close. Put your hand on my shoulder and watch where you put your feet."

"You don't have a flower name," muttered Sorrel. "You're not from Bana." Emrallie did not reply.

CHAPTER 14 – BIBI

My mother loved Sorrel from the moment she first held her. I think she gave her hope. How bad could anything be if babies were still being born? She chose her name. "She mustn't be soft, like a daisy or a rose. Call her Sorrel, something red and spiky. And December used to be the picking time for sorrel."

She held Sorrel in her arms and told her stories of the Convergence.

You should sing to her or tell her stories for babies, I would say, or talk about before when everything was better. But my mother only talked about what had happened. She said the Convergence was like an avalanche in cold countries, sweeping everything before it. Power cuts, then crash of the grid, followed by three years of darkness before solar panels brought electricity to homes. Ever new diseases. Failure of antibiotics. Collapse of water delivery systems. The relentless hurricanes, until the dust from a thousand deserts took to the air and shut down the hurricanes.

We rejoiced, she whispered to Sorrel, because there were no hurricanes, but we didn't realize how much water they brought. Six years of drought; the rivers dried up, fires raced up hillsides. And then the rain came back. Nobody had seen such rain, maybe a month's worth in an hour. A new name: rain bomb. Cities drowned. The forests fell, the trees simply fell over when the earth couldn't hold them. The soil washed off and turned the sea grey. The trade winds died. The white people, the rich people, left in panicked migrations for the north. The Renaming. The flower naming, of roads and airports and hotels and Domin buildings, as if changing the names of things could save us.

Then, The Fury.

My mother was beaten in the streets twice, just for being older.

Someone had to be blamed and it was the old people. She survived the beatings, one of which broke her arm in three places. She died when Sorrel was twelve, because she went looking for plums in a small, still-wooded valley in the foothills, where, it was rumoured, there was a bearing tree – she hated being inside all the time. Two days later she got the circular mark of the new tick disease, named the same as an old-time party on Bajacu. A *lyme*. We used to joke about the name, she told me, when the red circles on her arm appeared. I paid a cartman all the skynuts we had to take her body away, so Sorrel wouldn't see her. She always was close to her Grammy.

Sorrel walked behind Emrallie, touching her shoulder. The Tribal girl's hair tickled her wrist. Maybe she was fifteen or sixteen. The cave smelled musty and the Tribal carried no light. *No PlAK*, Sorrel thought suddenly. Maybe she had a bargaining tool after all.

There was a wavering light ahead and she began to see more of the large cave. She heard the murmur of voices and the sound of rushing water somewhere.

"Let me go now," Emrallie said, and Sorrel dropped her hand.

The Tribal led her into the light. A group of about ten females sat in a circle around a torch stuck in a receptacle. The light revealed brown faces under the same type of woven hat worn by Emrallie. Sorrel judged they were all teenagers.

One very tall girl had long black hair in a plait down her back. "Who's this?" she demanded, rising to her feet. She held a rusty shovel like a weapon. "Looks like a *guatan* Lowlander."

"She fell into the cenote. I pulled her out," Emrallie said.

"Why?" demanded the standing girl.

Emrallie shrugged. "She'd have drowned."

"She's got good boots," observed another with curly reddish hair. "You've got a real saviour complex, Emrallie."

"I've got a PlAK," blurted Sorrel and she felt the gaze of the Tribals. "A working PlAK. With a solar charger. We could go and get it when it's night. Also, two backpacks full of stuff."

"Why don't you have all this with you?" said the standing girl.

"She left it with her *mother*," Emrallie said.

"In the open?"

"Sounds like she was inside the culvert at Choreto Spring," Emrallie said. "I figure we should let Caroni decide what to do."

The standing female looked unconvinced. Sorrel saw one of the other girls put something in her mouth and she realised she was starving. "Do you have food?"

"Oh *guata*, Rashelope. Let her sit. Give her some food. We decide what to do nextnight," Emrallie said, taking Sorrel's elbow and pulling her into the circle of females.

They sat. One of the smallest girls picked up a strange round bowl and handed it to her. "Drink," she said. The liquid was nothing she had ever drunk before. It was so sweet it hurt her teeth. "Coconut water," said the girl. "I'm Lichen."

"She's probably never even seen a coconut," said the big female named Rashelope, who towered over Lichen.

"I thought they died off in the 60s," Sorrel said.

"There's a hybrid that survived in the mountains," Rashelope said. Her tone conveyed: *you clueless idiot.*

"Here, have some meat." Lichen handed her something wrapped in leaves. "What's your name?"

"You have *meat*?" Sorrel said, reaching for the food.

"Rodent... but yes, meat."

"My name is Sorrel," she said and all the Tribals laughed. She was too hungry to ask why. She stripped off the leaves and bit into the rodent. It was juicy and delicious with many small bones. The rodent was the opposite of alganola. Her head swam with exhaustion. She ate every bit of the meat, crunched the bones and licked her fingers. She eased herself out of the circle and, without permission, lay on the rocky floor of the cave. Her last thought was for Bibi, but her mother already seemed part of a different life.

She awoke to a blackness thick as oil. Fighting panic, she touched her eyes to make sure they were open. The torch was out, and the cave was silent. Her pants felt wet and she wondered if she had urinated in the night. Her stomach ached, a low cramping feeling. She thought then of menstrual periods. Hers had not started. Many girls never had periods now; they were too poorly nourished, too sedentary. There were those who said this was a good thing, because the lowered hormones in men and the barren women had brought human reproductive rates down, so there were more resources for everyone. Then the younger people

71

rebelled against supporting the older ones, and children became desirable again.

How would she cope if she got her period up here? Still, she wished for it, this marker into womanhood, especially up here, where she was outside Domin control.

She knelt and felt around her. She found the container which had held the coconut water and the scattered, greasy leaves the rodent had been wrapped in. She licked the leaves. They were gritty, but still had the taste of the meat. Perhaps the Tribals had abandoned her in the cave and she would never find her way out without light. "*Guata*," she yelled, to give herself courage. She swore again in anger and frustration. On all fours, she explored the place where she thought the Tribal females had sat and found the torch. If she could light it, perhaps she could find her way out.

"What're you screaming for?" Emrallie's voice came from behind her.

She turned with arms outstretched and touched the Tribal's face. Emrallie stepped back immediately.

"I thought you left me here to die," Sorrel said.

"We did consider it. You sure were sleeping. But, like I said, Caroni will decide. Come."

"Don't you need the torch?"

"No. Leave the torch here – might be needed in future."

"How do you light it?"

"Oh, there are still many things we use from the Lowlands. Matches are one of them. But your PlAK will have a magnifying glass – that's a useful tool, not easy to find these days. Put your hand on my shoulder and step where I step. We chipped away at this path," she said, sensing Sorrel's question. "Took months. But once you know where the edges are, they're easy to find with bare feet."

"Is it night?"

"Dusk."

It is cooler, Sorrel thought.

They came out of the cave into the evening. To see in this gentle light was a gift. The breeze was strong, and the leaves made soft sounds. Here was an older world. She took her hand from Emrallie's shoulder. "How far away is Caroni?"

"About two hours' walk."

"Emrallie. Please. We're closer to my mother. I wasn't running for ten minutes when I fell into that water. Let's get her. Let Caroni decide about both of us. We can get the packs and the PlAK. Please."

Emrallie glanced downward, then stared at her. "You got your period." Sorrel looked down and saw her pants were bloody. "That's gonna help you with Caroni. Is it your first time?"

"Yes."

"Probably happened because you were with a lot of females. We don't know why but we tend to bleed together. I'll show you the type of leaves we use. Do you have cramps?"

Sorrel heard a hint of sympathy in Emrallie's voice. "Cramps?" she said.

"Belly pain."

"Yes. I thought it was the rodent. Or the coconut water."

Emrallie laughed. "You really are a *guatan* babe in the woods. Let's wash out your pants by the cenote. Fill your algaskin. You won't mind being wet for a while. Then, okay, let's find your mother. You have some things going for you now. Not so much for her, though. If she's even alive."

They stood beside the cenote. "Where did this water come from?" she asked. "Why doesn't it evaporate?"

"It comes from underground. You heard it in the cave, right? This pool broke out in an earthquake a few years ago. The rocks fell in. Take your pants off, but don't put them in the cenote. That's drinking water." Emrallie untied one of the round vessels from her waist. It was stained red. "See that flat rock over there? Put your pants on it. Take water from the cenote with this. Beat your pants against the rock."

The pool had very steep sides – she couldn't see a way to get down to the water without falling in. She hesitated.

"Oh *guata*," Emrallie said. "Follow me." She pushed her way into a clump of bushes which hid the beginnings of a rocky path. She pointed. "Down there. We're lucky it's so steep. Stops the ferals from using it. Except for the avians. I'm going to look for *khaya* leaves. I'll be back."

Sorrel was relieved she was gone. She didn't want to be naked in front of Emrallie. Maybe getting her period meant she was fertile. Since the Domin Decree of 2076, females with periods had to report to the Domins and mate by lottery with a male of the Domin force. If such a female got pregnant, she was taken away by the Domins. No one knew what happened to those women after they had given birth, or to the babies.

Even outside Domin control, she wasn't sure she wanted to risk childbirth. Ever. She laughed a little at herself. Having a baby still needed a male.

She climbed down to the water as quickly as she could, but the path was treacherous, and she felt clumsy and slow. The blood washed out more easily than she'd anticipated and when she struggled into her pants, the wet clothes were heavy and soothing on her limbs. She washed her face and arms and filled her algaskin, drinking all it held, and filling it again. She climbed up the path to a flat rock, where she sat gazing at the pool below. Unlimited fresh water. She wished she could swim, like her mother. It was getting dark. Something flew out of the bushes and she ducked.

"A bat," Emrallie said, returning with a handful of soft brown leaves. "They survived in the mountains. Here. Put these in your pants. Split them in half. Keep the rest for later." She seemed to sense Sorrel wanted her to leave and she ran without hesitation down the steep path to the cenote. As she watched, Emrallie removed her hat and boots, then drenched herself with a light brown container, over and over. The filmy clothes clung to her long, smooth limbs and wide, sloping shoulders. She turned her squarish face to the evening sky and stood like that for a moment. Then she squeezed water out of her hair and replaced her boots, balancing easily on one leg, then the other, at the edge of the cenote.

"Right," she said, looking up at Sorrel. "Let's get your mother."

They stood under the culvert in the dark. "Bibi?" called Sorrel. Let her be alive, she whispered to herself.

"Oh, for earth's sake. Who could hear that? LOWLAND WOMAN! Come out if you're in there! Your daughter is here," Emrallie bawled. There was no reply.

"Are you going to look? Never mind. I'll do it." Emrallie pulled herself up and wriggled inside the culvert. Sorrel heard scraping sounds and then the Tribal's voice, but couldn't make out her words.

Emrallie slithered out. "She's there. But I'm not sure she can walk. Looks like she didn't drink anything – did you leave water with her?"

"'Course I did. Let me go in."

Sorrel climbed into the hole in the earth. She lay full length in the old culvert and waited for her night vision to come; then she reached forward with her hands and began feeling her way along the sides of her mother's hiding place.

Her hands touched the coarse material of one of the backpacks. She found the opening and began to feel around inside. "Bibi," she called. "Please answer me."

"One? Is that you?" Her mother's voice sounded like worn down machinery.

"It's me. Some Tribals found me. We have to go with them. What happened? Why can't you move?"

"Tribals?"

"Yes. Tribals. Come out. Turn on the PlAK." Sorrel tried to keep the impatience and worry out of her voice. She heard the whirr of the device and the culvert was flooded with light. Her mother lay on her side, half of her face in the dust.

"Give me your hand. Let's slide you out of here. I'll get the packs after."

After helping Bibi out, they stood outside, facing Emrallie. "This is my mother, Bibi," Sorrel said. "This is Emrallie. She saved my life. I fell into a pool and almost drowned."

"A pool?"

"A cenote," Emrallie said. "From an underground river."

"A river?"

"Are you going to repeat everything I say?" Emrallie demanded.

"Leave her alone," Sorrel said. She turned to her mother. "Did you drink?"

"Some."

"Well, drink some more now," Emrallie said. "I'm not going to slow down for either of you."

Bibi's head came up. "You don't have to slow down for anyone," she said to Emrallie. "Pass me the pack, Sorrel."

"I'll take your backpack, old woman."

"I carried it here, I'll keep carrying it," Bibi said.

"You do what I say, or I leave you both here."

"Who's using the old cable car farther down?" Sorrel said, trying to distract Emrallie.

"Lowland males. You don't want to be there when they come back. You're not the first to follow that old stream bed, but no one makes it to the end of the cable car line. There's a sheer drop off at the top – old landslide – and a huge pack of ferals. This male band has been here longer than most – they must have a source of food and water somewhere. We need to go."

Emrallie shouldered Bibi's pack and turned as if she didn't care whether they followed her or not. Bibi walked after her, moving stiffly, but benefiting from the absence of the pack's weight. Sorrel followed. The cramping in her lower abdomen seemed to pull her into the ground. She wanted to tell her mother she had got her period and that she was glad to find her alive, but Bibi was ahead of her, following a path that only the Tribal girl could see.

CHAPTER 16 – RAVINE

They strode through the night with the PlAK off. A fuzzy moon spilled an ungenerous light over the land. The Tribal girl moved at a silent, surefooted pace as if she could see in the dark. The Lowlanders dislodged pebbles, tripped on rocks and got caught by bushes, but together they moved steadily uphill, changing direction often. Sorrel had no idea where they were. She wished she could stare into the PlAK's screen, for its connection to the satellites which kept track of where things were.

She thought of her life in Bana, and her friend Sesame, almost certainly lost to her now. She wanted to tell her the Tribals were real. She thought of the sea-egg she'd shared with her mother on the day they joined the ranks of the displaced. She pushed away her anxiety and let the journey take her over.

"Right. Pay attention now." Emrallie had stopped. "We're going behind a boulder in a minute, and there'll be some ropes attached overhead. We have to rappel down a cliff. You wait until I'm down; then you follow."

"Rappel?"

Emrallie sighed. "Good thing you're wearing belts. I have string."

"String?"

"Turn on the PlAK. You'll need to see."

They stood on a ledge over a sheer cliff face descending into darkness. Emrallie had taken off a layer of the gauzy material and the Lowlanders saw she wore a kind of harness around her torso. She passed a rope fixed to something high above their heads which Sorrel couldn't see. Emrallie took the string from Sorrel and stretched it out to see how long it was. "Can work," she muttered. "*Guatan* lucky."

She tied the end of the string to her harness and handed the other to Sorrel. "When I get down, I'll take off the harness. You pull it up and put it on your mother. Lucky we're all about the same size. See this? It's a carabiner. Fasten it to the harness and send her down. Then we'll do it for you. Watch how I do it now." She tied and retied the rope several times through the metal clip she held. "Can you do that?" she asked.

"I think so."

"Don't step off the cliff unless the rope is holding you."

I don't think I can do this, thought Sorrel. She had never liked heights. She didn't look at Bibi, who was silent too.

"Give me the backpacks," Emrallie said, and Sorrel handed them over. "Is there anything that'll break inside?"

"The PlAK," Sorrel said.

"Give it to me."

Sorrel obeyed, wondering if she would ever see it again. Emrallie tied both packs together and threw them over the cliff. Sorrel did not hear them land. Then the Tribal tucked the PlAK under the harness, turned her back to the abyss and, as if it were the easiest thing in the world, stepped off the ledge.

"*Guata*," whispered Sorrel to herself. Emrallie bounced once off the cliff face and then disappeared into the blackness.

"Can you do this, Bibi?"

"We don't have a choice. She has all our stuff."

The rope went slack and swung towards her. "Pull up the harness!" Emrallie shouted. Her voice echoed, then died away.

The string brought up the harness and she put it on Bibi, cinching it as tight as it could go. She passed the rope through the metal clip, fighting the urge to do it over and over. She wouldn't know for sure when it was done right anyway. Without hesitation, Bibi turned her back to the cliff's edge and stepped off into the air. Sorrel heard her mother gasp as she hit the cliff face somewhere below. Emrallie shouted instructions to her but there was no reply.

Moments later, Emrallie yelled, "She's down!"

Sorrel pulled up the harness. She edged closer to the cliff, trying to take the strain off the rope by bending her knees. The rope held her, and she understood that the carabiner allowed her to go down at an even pace. She had no idea where such a device could be found. She stood at the edge and stared up at the cliff face, wondering how the Tribals came up from whatever was at the bottom and how her mother had stepped off into space so easily. The sky was becoming lighter.

"Hold the rope below you with your other hand! Let it out slowly. Come down in big jumps," shouted Emrallie.

She stepped off over the edge. Her eyes became level with the ledge she had been standing on. She pushed off again and the ledge disappeared overhead. With each jump she gained confidence and pushed off harder, calling out in exhilaration and triumph. "Slow down!" yelled Emrallie. Sorrel hit the ground hard and fell over.

"Fool!" Emrallie said. "You're lucky not to break a leg."

"That was amazing!" Sorrel laughed out loud and realised she had not laughed liked that in a long time. "How'd you learn how to do that?"

"Long story. Let's go. I'm tired."

They were in some kind of ravine. Sheer rock walls stretched above them. The air seemed wet and the sound of rushing water was deafening. For the first time in her life, Sorrel longed for daylight, so she could have a clear view of where she was.

Dawn came as they walked on, but it was far overhead. They were so deep in the ravine that it would probably be in shadow all day. There were real trees, with trunks and canopies and flowers, deepening the shadow thrown by the cliff walls. And there was a river at the very bottom of the ravine, blue and green and frothing white.

"Come along," Emrallie said. "Stop gawping. We still have to find shelter – might be no direct sun, but it's still going to heat up."

"I didn't know there were any rivers left," Sorrel said.

"Not surface ones, anyway. This was underground until the earthquake, like I said. We're not sure how long it will last – it's already got less water than before."

They followed Emrallie along a narrow, treacherous trail, slick with green plant growth. The air was full of spray from the river.

"Can we fill our algaskins?" Sorrel asked.

"Not here. Just follow me."

They had to slide down the last part of the trail. They were close to the river now and the noise made conversation impossible. Emrallie threaded her way through the trees which grew closer and closer together. The light was a green gloom and insects made scratching sounds around them. She heard the whine of mosquitoes and the faint chirp of a bird. Life rustled in the undergrowth and in the leaves – what remained, she thought, of a living world. Perhaps there were fish in the river, maybe even shrimp. If there were flowers, there would be fruit. The ground was stony, but there was soil; crumbly, black soil. She reached for her mother's hand and for the first time since they left Bana, Bibi smiled.

They could no longer see Emrallie – she was too far ahead.

"*Guata*, people, stop gazing!" Emrallie said, returning. "Come on!"

They emerged in a round clearing with a circle of small stones in the middle. The canopy above was unbroken. There was no one there and Sorrel wondered if this was just a resting place. As her eyes adjusted to the gloom, she saw shelters among the trees made of different materials – woven roofs, mud and stone walls, threadbare tarpaulins. Bamboo – split and laced into flat surfaces. Sheets of wood were made into lean-tos.

Now, the noise of the river was muffled, and the insect sounds came from a distance. "You'll have to share my hut," Emrallie said. "I hope you don't snore." She was looking at Bibi.

"You still sleep in the day?" Sorrel asked.

"Mostly. Sometimes we don't. But if we want to move around outside the ravine, we have to travel at night. Needs practice."

"How d'you get out of here?"

"We follow the river to where it disappears underground, near that cave we were in. There's a trail there. But it takes much longer. If we're being chased, we always use the cliff. Nobody follows us off there."

Sorrel didn't ask who might be doing the chasing.

They entered a small mud hut. Stones of many different sizes and colours studded the walls, along with bits of coloured glass.

The roof was made of interlaced bamboo and dried vines. There were no windows, just a gap between the walls and the roof for ventilation. The floor was dirt, packed hard. There was a stool in one corner, presumably from the Lowlands, and a pile of bedding in another. A hanging shelf made of wood held a line of algaskins, all full. A few articles of clothing hung on the hut's frame.

"Probably you want to change those leaves," Emrallie said to Sorrel. "I'll show you where we excrete – do it anywhere else and we throw you in a sinkhole. Don't think we can't. Or won't. Take a full algaskin with you. Use it all – there's no shortage of water here."

She led the way through the trees to another clearing with many trenches dug in the ground in a star pattern. Each one had an old shovel beside it and a pile of loose dirt. Some trenches had makeshift benches above them. "Wash up, drink, and then we sleep. Nextnight we speak with Caroni. Can you find your way back to the hut?"

"Yes," Sorrel said, although she wasn't completely sure. Every tree trunk looked the same. She relieved herself, threw the soiled leaves in one of the trenches and replaced them. They were soothing on her skin. The Tribals had to have a deep knowledge of the world to live like this. She picked up the shovel and covered the soiled leaves.

Even deep in the forest the heat was growing. She washed her hands and face and poured the rest of the water from the algaskin on her head. She looked across to her mother, who was using one of the distant benches over a trench. When she had finished, they made their way together back to the hut.

Sorrel and Bibi were alone. "I got my period," Sorrel said.

"Really, One?"

"Yes. Emrallie showed me what to do. My belly hurts though."

Bibi reached out her arms and Sorrel walked into her mother's embrace.

CHAPTER 17 – ZORAH

She slept the entire day. It had been hot, but not dangerously so. She'd been aware of Emrallie leaving the hut and had heard the far-off sounds of voices and movements outside. When she finally woke, her body was filmed with sweat and the day was dying. Bibi was still asleep beside her. She had mud on her cheek, and her face looked crumpled like used paper.

Sorrel stood and stretched. Their backpacks were against the wall of the hut, but the PlAK was gone. *We're at the mercy of the Tribals now*, she thought. They were more than capable of throwing them both into the river, or a sinkhole, as Emrallie had threatened, or simply chasing them away to stumble around in the forest. She reached for one of the algaskins and drained the contents. She was ravenous.

She walked out of the hut and saw many young females of different ages carrying out various tasks, some sitting in the circle of stones she had seen earlier, others on stools in front of their shelters, bent over containers. No one met her eyes. She remembered the rodent and her mouth watered.

"We thought you would sleep through the night as well," Emrallie said from behind her.

"Where's the PlAK?"

"The Zorah has it. Time you met her now. Wake your mother."

"She's really tired."

Emrallie looked irritated. "Of course she is."

"Can we at least wash first?" she said.

"Yes. I'll wait for you here. Don't forget to take water with you."

Sorrel and Bibi went to the clearing with the trenches, where they saw other women and girls pouring water for baths and wielding shovels. No one looked at them or said anything. They were probably waiting on the Zorah's decision too. Bibi walked a short distance away to a trench no one was using.

The Tribal females were mostly teenagers and very young adults. The big female from the cave was the only one with long hair; everyone else's – a variety of textures and colours – was cropped to chin length. Their body hair was not shaved. Their limbs were muscular. They wore a mishmash of clothing – pants, skirts, shorts, long dresses, sleeveless tops, floaty blouses – the same gauzy material Emrallie wore, and they stripped down to the skin without embarrassment, hanging their clothes on the trees and bushes. Their skins were shades of brown and red. Some had limbs made darker by the sun and she could see tan lines at their wrist and neck. Others were obviously more careful about exposure to the sun and were one, smooth colour. She thought they would normally have been speaking with each other, laughing perhaps, but it was clear that their presence silenced them. These females live or die together, she thought. How had they found each other? Where were their families?

Her belly pain had stopped. She used the last of the leaves and wondered where they could be gathered. Bibi came back looking much cleaner and stronger. Together, they returned to Emrallie's hut, where she was waiting.

Emrallie led them farther away from the clearing with the stone circle as night closed in. Sorrel heard the calls and rustles of night creatures and had no way of knowing whether they helped or harmed humans. Mosquitoes whined around her ears and she waved them away, wondering about fevers. Bats carried viruses and rodents had ticks. Despite these dangers, the night air was almost cool on her skin and a sense of wellbeing flooded her body.

Emrallie led them to a hut like all the others, which surprised Sorrel, who thought surely the Zorah would have the biggest shelter. A wiry woman with straight, dark hair sat on a stool in front of the entrance beside the PlAK. There was a fat candle under a glass dome beside her – Sorrel had seen those in Bana. Her face was half in shadow, but she had lines in her forehead and looked older than thirty-five.

The woman stood when they approached, and Sorrel felt awkward – how should she greet the leader of the Tribals?

"I hear you're Lowlanders," the woman said. "I won't say welcome yet. My name is Caroni and I'll hear your story." There were two other stools nearby, which looked like they were the cut trunks of trees.

"Hello," Sorrel began, meeting the Zorah's eyes. "I'm Sorrel. From Bana. This is my mother, Bibi and –"

"Wait. In good time. I'm sure you're hungry. Let's eat first and then we'll talk. Come. Emrallie, you can leave us."

Caroni led the Lowlanders behind the hut, where there was a low, round stove, full of glowing, ashy wood. She pulled out something wrapped in broad, serrated leaves and put it on a large, flattish rock. "River fish," Caroni said, opening the steaming packet. "Cross between a tilapia and a catfish. They hybridized sometime way back. See the big eyes? They can survive without much light in underground water. Whoa, wait. Be careful not to burn your fingers. I'd let it cool a little."

There was a black orb on the top of the stove. "Breadfruit," Caroni said. "We found an old tree high up. Have you ever eaten it?" She spoke to Sorrel, ignoring Bibi.

Sorrel shook her head. She had read about breadfruit in the History module but never seen the tree or the fruit. The orb looked industrial rather than edible, but it smelled wonderful. Her mouth filled with saliva. She didn't want to admit that she had rarely eaten fish and had never heard of tilapia or catfish. She half-wondered if a catfish was some form of feral, made by a feline and a piscine, but surely lungs could not become gills, or vice versa. No, that was stupid.

Caroni knelt in front of the flat rock for a moment, almost as if in prayer. She juggled the breadfruit and skilfully peeled off the black skin with a knife. The flesh inside was a pale steaming yellow. She sliced it into rough quarters and handed a quarter to Sorrel on the tip of the knife. "Let it cool," she reminded her. Then she gave a smaller piece to Bibi.

Sorrel unwrapped the fish and the flesh fell away from the bones. "Let the breadfruit soak up the juices," Caroni said, and Sorrel watched how the woman ate the food, pulling the fish apart and laying the breadfruit on top of the flesh. There were other types of vegetables in the leaf packet, things Sorrel had only ever read about – onions, potatoes, carrots and tiny tomatoes. She burned her fingers and mouth. The fish was firm and only slightly muddy to the taste, but the breadfruit – oh she had never eaten anything like that roasted breadfruit! Firm and thick and full of juice. *Real*, she thought.

When they had finished, Caroni held her algaskin over Sorrel's hands and poured a trickle of water; then they reversed positions. She indicated that Sorrel should do the same for her mother. "Now, let's talk," she said, leading them back to the front of the hut. She picked up her stool and the candle and they went inside.

Caroni pointed to a log and looked directly at Sorrel. "Let's hear your story."

"Shouldn't we bring the PlAK inside?" Sorrel said.

"Why?"

"Someone might take it?"

Caroni laughed. "No one will take it, Lowlander. Talk."

Where to start? Perhaps with good manners. "Thank you for the delicious food. I've never eaten anything like that."

"It's hard-won. Perhaps you'll find that out for yourself. Now, why are you here?" Caroni's small welcoming smile was gone.

"Well. There's not much to say. We lived in Bana and we moved around, like everybody else. The Immersion Zone kept changing. Then our house was included in the zone and we got an Evacuation Order. I couldn't sleep in the day. Ever. And I just didn't want to live like that. So we decided to try for the mountains." It sounded like the flimsiest of stories. "We didn't know if Tri – I mean, you – really existed."

"How did you come upon the cable car line?"

"We looked for routes using the PlAK's SATMAP and found the dry stream bed, which led to the water tank and the columns. My mother thought it was a good direction to take. We spent a night in the tank. Then followed the columns upwards. Emrallie told us others did the same thing."

"You have access to the PlAK's SATMAP?"

"Yes." She nodded in Bibi's direction, annoyed at the way she was being ignored. "My mother worked at the tech centre and has Level 3 info-clearance. You could ask her about it."

"I'm asking you. But that *is* interesting. We had a PlAK once, but no one here could access higher than Level 4. The SATMAP would be really helpful."

"There's a whole heap you can do with Level 3 clearance," Bibi said. "And a lot with an old PlAK. Did you keep it?"

Caroni didn't acknowledge her. "Why'd you leave your mother in the culvert?" she asked Sorrel.

"We saw footprints in the cable car and were afraid to stay there. I found a trail. Wanted to see where it led, but day was coming. I could run, and she couldn't."

No one said anything more. Caroni looked at her hands.

"What's going to happen to us? Will you let us stay?" Sorrel's voice shook.

"I don't know yet." The Zorah turned to Bibi. "How old are you?"

"Forty-five." Her voice was strong and almost defiant.

Caroni shook her head. "We don't keep old people. Everyone has to leave the band at forty. Even me."

"Why?" Sorrel asked.

"Old people need care. Takes too much out of the young. Triage – do you know that word?"

"She has the info-clearance," Sorrel said.

"We've managed without a working PlAK for a long time," Caroni said. "It's tempting, though."

"Old people know things. They have wisdom. Experience." Sorrel felt her mother's eyes on her.

"Maybe, yes. But this world asks more of the body than the mind."

The Zorah lapsed into silence again. The candle flickered, and Sorrel's hope started to ebb.

"Can I ask you some questions now?" she said.

"Go ahead."

"Will you kill us?"

"Not directly. We'd take you down to Burning Rock Plain and leave you there. You wouldn't last a day."

"That's cold."

Caroni stared at her. "The opposite of cold."

"I'd rather drown."

The older woman shrugged. "Could be arranged. We don't like dead bodies in the river, but… Anyway, ask your questions. I've got things to do before daybreak."

"What is this place?"

"A ravine. We call it Jiba. The river was underground before, but we think the roots of the trees and plants could still reach the water, so they grew tall. Insects and birds came. Then ferals. The river broke out in an earthquake. We found it by accident – one of us, Lane, fell down the cliff. We were looking for the river – we could hear it. Lane died, of course."

"What d'you call the river?"

"Sacred."

"How long have you been a band?"

"Six years, maybe. Not always the same people. I've been Zorah for three."

"Are you all female?"

"Yes. Males bring complications. Violence. But there are a few bands with males and females, and some with all males. There are far fewer males born now. Anyway, we try to avoid them."

"Do you grow food?"

"Some. Potatoes, carrots. Some we trade with other bands. Some we forage. The breadfruit was from a single tree. We think we're the only ones to find it so far. Onions don't grow up here – that was a trade. You'll have seen the skynut trees. Sometimes we catch fish or birds. We've started drying insects too. And fruit."

"Fruit?"

"Mangoes. Plums."

"You live up here with nothing from the towns?"

"Not nothing. We scavenge and trade. Some of us are from those towns. Sometimes we get things from buried towns too. Is that it?"

"How did you find each other?"

"Some of us are – were – the mothers and children the Domins held after the women got pregnant for men in the Squad. They escaped, stayed together. Some found us, like you did, but in other places. No one has found Jiba until now."

"Some of you never had families?" Bibi asked.

"Some never did. Some don't remember. Others lost theirs in

a dozen different ways. Now we are a tribe, not a family. It's a different thing. We look after each other. If there's conflict, I have to decide for the good of everybody."

"How old are you?"

"Thirty-five."

"What happened to your family? How can you talk so easily about putting us out to die?"

Caroni's eyes shone in the flickering light. "I don't tell my story to strangers."

"What about when it's your time?" Bibi said.

Caroni shrugged. "I don't know if I'll survive ten years. I don't know if I'll survive next week."

"When will you decide about us?" Sorrel asked.

"Nextnight."

"Suppose we just walk away from the camp?"

"Better than the Burning Rock Plain, I imagine. But the band will probably want to find you."

"We're no threat to you."

"You are. If you survive, you'll tell about this ravine with the river. If the Toplanders or Domins catch you, they'll make you talk."

"About the Toplanders… are they real?"

"Very real."

"Is it true they capture Lowlanders for slaves?"

"Yes, they're at Cibao. We've never been there – hard to find somewhere better than Jiba. We've heard about the slaves – well, more than that. Rashelope found a girl who'd escaped from the Toplanders once. Every finger was broken, she was blinded in one eye. She died before Rashelope could get too much from her. She kept saying a word no one understood. Drax. Drax. They're brutal, the Toplanders. Worse than the Domins."

There was a longer silence.

"To get this straight – " Bibi began, but the Zorah interrupted.

"No more questions. Go back to Emrallie's hut. Sleep, if you like to sleep in the night. Might be your last."

"I've slept enough. Caroni? Can I call you Caroni?"

"Yes. Go and rest now."

"How can we rest? You may put us out when day comes."

"Daylight can kill you any day," Caroni said.

Back in Emrallie's hut, Sorrel lay staring at the roof. She heard the rush of the river and the turmoil of the forest and it was like music. Emrallie was not in the hut, but the bedding had been shaken out and there was a full algaskin left for each of them.

Bibi sat, leaning against the hut walls. A faint glow from the candles and torches the Tribals held filtered through the gap between the walls and roof of the hut. Sorrel liked it better than the harshness of the streetlights in Bana. A waft of warm, wet air drifted through the door and feathered her skin. Her stomach was full of good food. She had slept for almost eight hours in the day. She turned to Bibi.

"What d'you think? Should we just leave now and take our chances?"

"I don't think so, One. This is a good place. It's what you wanted, isn't it?"

"But they could take us to the Burning Rock Plain when daylight comes."

"I doubt they will. That head woman – Caroni – wanted my info-clearance. We should rest now." Bibi avoided her daughter's eyes. "Lie down."

"I've slept enough. You rest."

Sorrel stared into the dark, thinking about a possible escape. Probably the PlAK was still attached to its charger outside Caroni's hut and she could retrieve it. They had their backpacks. They could fill as many algaskins as they could carry from the river. Maybe she could find her way to the river in the dark, but then what? Perhaps they could follow it until it disappeared into the earth, but could they find their way back to the culvert, back to the cable car columns and even then, what about the landslides at the top and the feral pack Caroni had described or the band of Lowlander males who used the cable car? The brutal Toplanders? Her mother's tiredness?

She looked over at Bibi who was turned away. Her body did not have the relaxed look of sleep and her breathing was quiet. Sorrel got up and walked out into the forest, touching the trees as she went, making sure she could still see the camp. She knew what her mother would say – *We need a plan.*

Could they throw themselves into the river, until they found a place they could crawl out? The water would take them far and fast, and surely if the band had found their way out of the ravine, they could too. Then she remembered her desperate fight for breath and the light at the surface of the cenote pool as she sank, until Emrallie had reached down and saved her.

Bibi could swim, though. Maybe there was something they could hold onto like the many fallen tree limbs at the river's edge. The river could let them travel by day, which no one would expect. She imagined a calm pool, far downstream, sheltered by rocks or a fallen tree, where they could stay partly submerged and therefore hidden for most of the day. They would be hungry, but they would have water. Maybe they could catch a fish and eat it raw. The PlAK would probably be destroyed by water but the river was surely better than the Burning Rock Plain. She would be with her exhausted mother in an unfamiliar world once again and they would have to search for shelter every day. She felt her spirit quail.

She wanted to stay with the Tribals. They had clearly warmed towards her but seemed to have rejected Bibi. Triage. Could Caroni be right? That this new world demanded a hard heart and a willingness to shed attachments?

She tried to separate her fate from her mother's, but the thought made her want to wail.

You and me against the world.

Some members of the band seemed to be getting ready to leave the clearing. She knew so little about how they lived. The girl, Lichen, who had been kind to her in the cave, waved shyly.

She turned to go back to the hut. *We just have to convince them we're both useful. Show them what Bibi can do with the PlAK.*

It was dark inside, and her eyes took a moment to adjust. "Bibi?" she called softly, but the low shape did not move. The hut was silent. She knelt to touch her mother's shoulder, but the pile of bedding was empty.

Drew loved his child, called her a miracle in the mess. He read a lot about other times when civilization failed. We used to fight over the PlAK, which was where he got his information. He wouldn't let me breast feed Sorrel alone in the night, got up with me every time. This is a one-person task, I would say.

I feel like I'm feeding her too, he'd reply.

Sorrel grew – I'd even say she thrived. I told myself that she would adapt to the world she was born into. Alganola would be food and she would never long for the Sunday lunch of my grandparents' generation. I was wrong. There were a thousand ways to learn of everything that had been lost – my mother's stories, school, the internet. Her genetics spoke to her too.

My daughter's face caused guilt and fear to rise in me in equal measure. I read that when an organism is threatened, it reproduces; determined to pass on its genes into the future. My mother used to talk about how the fruit trees went in for an orgy of bearing just before they died. I was an animal, after all. We all are.

As food got more and more scarce, Drew began to collect weapons; well, it is more accurate to say he began to fashion them. He could make anything. He made machetes and axes and spears – mostly implements for cutting and stabbing. He'd heard the tech centre had a 3D printer for making guns, but he never found it.

What are you going to do with these? I asked him, as the axes piled up under our bed. Knives would be more useful. Make some knives. He made another axe, his face gone so thin it was like a knife. Sometimes he went outside at night and practised with the weapons he had made, fighting an enemy only he could see.

Of course, I asked him why he cut down the skynut tree. Why not just the nuts?

I had to see if what I made would work, he said. The axe worked like a dream.

Why not cut a tree with no fruit?

The nuts were high, he said, and I couldn't reach them, couldn't climb up. We were all hungry. One of us working wasn't enough.

I always knew when he was lying to me. Tell me the truth, I said, that first time I saw him in jail after his arrest.

I just wanted to swing at something, he confessed. Destroy a living thing. Take what I could. Like so many others did. I did it for us, and I'd done it before, they probably told you. Skynuts last for a long time; it's not like they would have wasted.

I saw the hopelessness and despair in his eyes.

When the Domins came they found all his axes, machetes and spears and that made things worse for him. They took them all away, except the knife we carried with us from Bana, the one Sorrel killed the feral canine with. They'd missed that one.

I pretended to be asleep in the hut. I knew my daughter would not sit for long. As soon as she left, I walked out behind her. I took only what I could tie to my body, and one of the filmy garments the Tribals wore. The sound of the river guided me out of the camp. I could swim, but it's easy to drown in a strong river.

To keep me company, I talked to Drew in my mind. I'd never seen his prison cell. When I used to visit, they would bring him to me in a concrete room with peeling paint and low benches. I never told him goodbye when we left Bana, but I know he would have said: go. We agreed long ago we would do whatever was necessary to keep our daughter safe.

I hesitated on the riverbank. Sacred, the Zorah had named the river. Maybe a judgment, maybe a name. The water was dark with curls of white around rocks or branches. I wondered whether I should take off my boots. They would weigh me down but protect my ankles. I left them on and waded into the cold water, near a fallen branch. I jumped down feet first, protecting my head from the rocks.

The current pulled and I didn't want to let go of the branch, but I knew Sorrel would not be long outside the hut and I was sure she'd look for me when she saw me gone. I didn't have a plan, I didn't have a destination, I didn't have the PlAK. All I knew was the river would take me away and I could stay in the water during the day.

I breathed as deeply as I could, then I let go.

CHAPTER 19 — SECOND CAVE

"So, she left," Caroni said.

"Looks so," Sorrel said. She stood with Emrallie in Caroni's hut. It hadn't taken the band long to discover Bibi's tracks down to the river.

"She knew I would let you stay, but not her. She made the decision for you," Caroni said.

"You're *guatan* heartless."

"I'm sorry for your loss. But it's best it happened this way."

"What's going to happen to me?"

"Nextnight, like I said."

"Why is everything nextnight?"

"We like to consider things without too much emotion. Emrallie, take the Lowlander to the cave cell. We'd have to go after her if she ran now." She turned to Sorrel. "I'm sorry to have to restrain you. Use the time to grieve."

"Please don't lock me up." Sorrel gave up trying to hold back her tears.

"You'll be comfortable. The cave is cool right through the day. I'll let you take the PlAK and there'll be food and water. Even a coconut. We're not cruel, but I must look after the others. Twelve hours and you'll be out." Caroni turned away.

Emrallie held her arm above the elbow. Sorrel shook her off.

"Don't make things harder," Emrallie said.

Outside Caroni's hut, Emrallie handed her the PlAK but not the charger. Then she led Sorrel away from the trees and the huts and into another narrow cave with weathered planks of wood across the entrance. She pulled out two of them. "Go inside. The PlAK will give you light after nightfall. There's a bucket for waste."

"I thought you would be my friend," Sorrel said.

"You don't know me. Caroni is a good Zorah. She'll do the right thing, you'll see. I'm sorry about your mother, but forty-five…" Her voice trailed off. She gave Sorrel a little push into the cave and hammered the wood back in place. Through the gaps between them, Sorrel could still see Emrallie's shape.

"My mother was the one who put me out," Emrallie said, her face close to the planks.

"I want my backpack," Sorrel said.

"Nextnight," Emrallie said. She turned and walked away.

Sorrel sank to the floor of the cave near the nailed-up entrance. She breathed in the outside air, stared at the lighter darkness of the forest. The floor of the cave was dry and smooth, as if it had been created by water. She lay down, knees to chest.

After a few minutes, she decided she was not a child and sat up and pulled the PlAK onto her lap. She turned on the light and swung it around the small cave, then got to her feet to find the spot where the signal was best. She sat and looked at last for Sesame's message.

"Where are you?" her friend had written, along with a string of emojis.

She learned that Sesame's family had disobeyed the mandatory evacuation order, because her mother didn't think she could walk anywhere – she had not left the house in years. Sesame and Bracken were planning to leave her behind. Triage.

Sesame was not online, but Sorrel wrote back, telling of their journey. "You were right, Ses. There are Tribals in the mountains. If you find the cable car line, maybe you can join us. Take your PlAK with you. I don't know about Bracken, though. There are no males here." She wanted to tell her about Bibi's departure, but the words wouldn't come.

She used the PlAK until the battery died. The signal was intermittent, and the screen froze often, but the SATMAP found a narrow stripe of green at over 2000 metres north of Bana, and she thought it had to be Jiba. There was no sign of the river. Presumably the image had been taken before it broke out. She wondered why more people had not found the ravine and decided that it was perhaps because they were not able to rappel down the cliff, and the other entrance was far away or hidden.

The SATMAP showed the ravine was not that far from the old army base at Cibao, where the rich people lived. The layers showing altitude indicated steep slopes and huge brown cutaways from many landslides, turning Cibao into a virtual fortress. The mountain looked as if it had been chewed and clawed at by a gigantic beast. The camp appeared deserted, but that meant nothing. Bana looked the same as the day they left – she would not know what had happened until weeks had passed.

She came upon message boards about the mountains – people claiming to have made it there, saying there was abundant food and cool temperatures. There were also stories of massacres by Tribals, attacks by ferals, and armies controlled by Toplanders. And a word, perhaps a name: Drax.

During that night, Sorrel reflected how even she had let herself believe, a little at least, in the information held by the servers in places far away. The only thing she could be sure of was what she was now experiencing. Her mother was gone, her father in prison, her home destroyed, her future owned by a group of strangers. She closed the PlAK. There was nothing to do but wait for Caroni's decision, hoping it would come at dawn. The Zorah had told her that the cave would be cool throughout the day. That probably meant that she had at least a day to wait.

COMMUNITY

2085

CHAPTER 20 – BREADFRUIT TREE

Emrallie and Sorrel ran along the wide bank of the river, now reduced to a thin, sluggish stream. Dawn was coming. The sandy bottom of the ravine was visible, full of large smooth rocks, carved by the river that had once risen up the sheer walls of the ravine. They had been sent by Caroni to pick the last breadfruits, regardless of their ripeness, before the sun was fully up. Everyone knew they had to leave the ravine, but no one knew when or where they would go. Every day the big trees shed more and more of their leaves and the ground crackled underfoot as the leaves turned to dust. Sunlight had started to reach the valley floor, first as dappling, then in expanding, irregular shapes. Slowly the Tribals stopped most activities during the day, except tree climbing, which needed daylight.

"Just round this bend," Emrallie said from in front. The Tribals had celebrated Emrallie's earthstrong day last week – she was sixteen, a year older than Sorrel, and now considered an adult woman. No one had asked when Sorrel's birthday was, and her fifteenth had passed a month before without notice. But she knew Bibi wouldn't have forgotten and, on that night, she had lit a candle for her mother. Rashelope had bawled at her for doing it – candles were running out. Everything was running out.

They had stayed at Jiba too long, Emrallie told her. "We're all too soft now. We've forgotten how to travel. How to do without."

They stared up at the breadfruit tree – there were only a few fruits left and they were very high. "Scout around for a long stick," Emrallie said. "Try over there in the bamboo clump."

It was almost a year since Sorrel had left Bana with her mother, almost a year since Bibi had gone. The Tribals had searched the banks of the river but had never found any trace of her – no blood on a rock, no body, none of her possessions. The chances of Bibi's survival were slim, but Sorrel still talked to her in her mind as she composed herself for sleep. She wanted to thank her for her sacrifice, for saving her from having to choose. She often wondered if she would ever feel love like that.

"You never stop daydreaming," Emrallie complained from the lowest crook of the breadfruit tree. "You found a stick yet?"

"Coming!" She was tired all the time now – her sleeplessness had returned. *Dooley.* Bibi had taught her that word to describe a mind made distracted and fuzzy by lack of proper sleep. She pushed her way into the dead bamboo grove. Some of the trunks on the ground crumbled as soon as she trod on them, and hordes of insects scattered. The ground under the fallen bamboo was damp and mosquitoes rose in clouds. She had got fever once in the past year, but with no lasting effects.

She wrestled with a slightly green stick of bamboo that was still standing at an acute angle and got it out of the ground. Its roots were shallow – it was not really suited to clinging to the sides of mountains. In the distant past, bamboo would not have been on Bajacu at all.

She stripped the branches, except those at the top, working quickly to avoid being accused of daydreaming again. Like Emrallie, she wore the filmy material, which she now knew came from parachutes stolen by Rashelope from the Bana air wing of the military. Her hair was chin-length and often full of twigs and leaves. All the Tribals except Rashelope kept their hair off their shoulders for coolness. She had a machete slung across her back, just as Emrallie had carried when they first met. Her most valuable possession was a gift from her friend – a pair of gloves with the fingers cut off.

"Get the breadfruit you can reach first," she shouted up to Emrallie. "Edge yourself in. Then I'll pass the bamboo."

"*Guata*, you're bossy," Emrallie responded, but she went higher. She was the best climber in the band. The breadfruits were small and green and dispersed all over the tree. Emrallie reached a few and was able to pick them by hand, but the rest took many attempts before she knocked them free with the pole. With each strike, the large, serrated leaves of the tree rained down. Its time was ending too.

Afterwards, they sat in the patchy shade to rest. The sun was up but they had an hour before they needed to be inside one of the huts in the camp. Sorrel thought the tough green breadfruits would be more useful as weapons than food. She remembered the first time she had tasted it on her first night in the Tribal camp. *Their* first night.

"What was it like, being always on the move, with this many people?' she asked Emrallie.

"Hard, although there were not so many of us then. Finding shelter every night, the ferals, dust storms, rain bombs. But it is cooler up here, so even when we were caught in the day, only a few died. But you know how it is…" She fell silent.

"When do you think we'll leave?"

"*Guata*, Sorrel. How many times you gonna ask the same question? I don't know. But I'll tell you this – all of us can't travel together for long. We're a big band because we had the camp and the river – Is that a fish down there?"

There was a small flapping creature on the riverbank, well before reproductive age. According to Tribal rules the only animals they could kill were the mature ones. "Should I throw it back in?" Sorrel asked.

"You crazy? Go get it. It's at least a bite each."

"Are we taking it back to camp?'

"What d'you think?" Emrallie was scornful. "Cooked or raw, is all I want to know."

"Best not to start a fire here."

"Probably the last roasted fish we'll ever eat. They'll all be inside at camp. Find some stones." She looked at the fish. "Doesn't even look like it's worth cleaning. You going to get it or not?"

"Fine, I'll go. You get the stones."

"I picked the breadfruit."

The dry breadfruit leaves on the ground were good kindling and they made a fire in a small hole lined with river stones. They tamped down the fire, wrapped the tiny fish in a few green leaves and laid it on the hot stones. They didn't give it enough time to cook and the fish was part raw. "Four bites each, I guess," Emrallie said, taking the first one. "You can have the head."

After they had sucked every bone dry, they cleaned their hands in the wet river sand. "We shouldn't go close to anyone when we get back," Sorrel said. "We smell of fish."

"Let's bathe then."

Sorrel glanced at the sky. "No point. We'll get dirty and sweaty on the way back."

"You don't get it, do you? After we leave, there'll be no huts. No river, so no water. No food a lot of the time. And we'll *never* be alone." Emrallie began to strip.

There was no depth to the river, but they would be able to lie in it. She undressed, no longer self-conscious. For the Tribals, all that mattered was body function – strength, agility and speed. Emrallie had no tan marks and liked to take off her clothes when it was safe. Sorrel envied Emrallie's ability to inhabit the present moment completely. She lay back in the water now, her eyes closed behind her dark glasses.

In her time with the Tribals, she'd learned their stories. Caroni's father was in the Domin Squad, so she'd been taken away from her mother as a baby. She'd grown up in one of the Domin camps and rarely saw her father. She'd seen some of the violence training and other kinds of training – how to find food, make a camp, track and hide. There were other children there. "I guess you could say we raised ourselves," she'd said without emotion.

"How did you leave?" Sorrel had asked.

"How? Or why?"

"Why, I guess."

"If you got a period, you were given to a Domin man. I saw those girls; they had nothing in their eyes."

Emrallie and Rashelope had been alone in the mountains the longest. Emrallie came from a big family and her father and youngest sister had been killed in a hurricane. They lived in a small town in the middle of the island and after the crops died and the roads buckled, there was no food. Her mother had taken them all on the move, looking for a place to settle. She'd learned survival skills at a young age, but there was never enough to eat.

Her mother had sacrificed her two youngest children – Emrallie and her brother, Teal. "We were triaged," she told Sorrel. "We were the weakest and needed the most care. We were a drain on the others. She chose from the bottom up. I don't blame her for it."

"What happened to Teal?"

"He died. We found shelter in a ruin – just a pile of square stones, must have been from really long ago. But a feral got him while I was out looking for food. He was six."

"You found his body?"

"I found the porcine eating him. One of those bigger ones with tusks. I killed it, hacked it up and ate it for a few days, but the flesh went bad really quickly. Kept the tusks as weapons for a long time, but they reminded me, so…"

"*Guata*, Em, that's awful. You had to bury your brother…"

"I didn't bury him. Waste of energy. Pulled him into the open and left him. He was dust in a week." She sighed. "Then I was alone. Eventually joined up with people on the move; and came up here. Left them, then I was alone again for a while, then with another group of Tribals – males and females. That was a disaster; and then I met Caroni." Her voice had fallen to a whisper.

"Why was the male band a disaster?"

"I don't really want to talk about it."

"D'you ever wonder what happened to your mother and your siblings?"

"Not anymore."

"I still mi… aahm, think about my mother."

"After all this time? For what? She'd be weak and need looking after. Put us all at risk."

"You're hardhearted," Sorrel had said and regretted the words immediately.

"You think so? I tell you who's hardhearted. Those old people, dead now. They left us this world to deal with and they *knew* what would happen. But they kept right on with their meat every day and their homes with rooms no one went into and their holidays. I hate every generation before this one, more than the Domins. I hate it that I'll never have a chance to confront them."

The river had been cold when it was deep – now it was warm as blood. The gravel of the stream bed shifted slightly beneath Sorrel's body, accommodating her weight. Emrallie said she had been with a male band for a while. Sorrel thought about being touched by someone else. A male. Touched intimately. She knew a few of the older females were lovers, but her new, unwelcome dreams were of bodies different from hers. Boys. Men. These dreams seemed to flow out of her body, not her mind.

"D'you ever think of boys now?" she asked Emrallie.

She said nothing for a long while, then said, "Think of them how?"

"Being with them. Touching them."

"Having sex, you mean?"

"I guess."

"No. I don't think of them. Males are dangerous. And it's too much of a risk. I'm fertile, at least I used to be."

"Don't you want children?"

"Children? To have a baby? To be torn apart from the inside? Up here? And then see them die? For *what*?"

"Will humans die out then? The things that reproduce survive. Like the ferals."

"You think too much, Sorrel. I don't think about *humanity*. I think about how much of this breadfruit I'm gonna get, if it can be eaten at all. If I'll ever lie in a river again, or if it'll be back to licking the underside of rocks and sucking on agaves. Whether we'll find a good place – no, *any* place – when we leave Jiba. I don't think about *males*."

The earth shook slightly, and a few stones rolled off the cliffs. There were tremors all the time now.

CHAPTER 21 – AMERIKANS ARE COMING

The Zorah called a band meeting that night. There was little food. Rashelope had found a cache of alganola in an abandoned cabin lower down the mountain and they ate some of it. The breadfruits were stored in one of the empty huts, wrapped in leaves, to give them the best chance of ripening. Sorrel looked around. Everyone was too thin. Most sat alone, their eyes lowered. Only Rashelope still bled every month. At least all the algaskins were full. Sorrel grimaced at the thought of sucking the underside of rocks, of the gelatinous texture of the inner flesh of agave.

Rashelope always spoke first at band meetings – she was their eyes and ears. No one except Caroni knew her story. She was almost 183 centimetres tall and her shoulders were square and strong. She moved through the bush as if on wings. She knew every old road and faint trail to every destroyed town in this part of the island, all the way back to Bana. She navigated the streets of the dying capital city like a wraith. She led a small band of the youngest girls who did whatever she asked. She was the one who brought new members to the band, but there had not been anyone new in months.

"The market is bone dry," she said. "Nobody has anything to trade or sell. The dump at Oconuco is cleaned out. And the drones are back; dozens of them. The roads are full of Squaddies – I don't know where they're finding fuel for their ATVs. We couldn't get anywhere near Bana this trip – nobody's coming out either. We'll starve if we stay here." She knelt, looking worried. Before, Sorrel had never seen Rashelope look anything but fierce.

Lichen stumbled to her feet. She was one of Rashelope's roving band; not strong, but small and nimble with a talent for hiding. She hardly ever spoke at band meetings. "Th-there's talk," she stammered.

"What kind of talk?" Caroni said. "Speak up, Lichen."

"T-talk of an invasion from outside. P-people coming here. Northerners."

"People from off the *island*? Why, though? There's no food here and the sea is rising."

"We still have m-mountains. T-trees in a few places. Water underground." She pointed to what was all around them. "No w-winter. The big countries – they're b-burning all the time, even in cold places. Better air here, when there's no d-dust."

"Rashelope? Did you hear this too?"

"No. But I trust Lichen. She listens."

"Where did you hear this, Lichen?"

"At the O-Oconuco dump. We were just leaving when I heard voices, so I hid. Some tech p-people came, looking for spare p-parts. They had an argument – some of them wanted to tell the tech b-bosses that they had seen this invasion on a server, but the others said it would only get them into t-trouble because that server was off limits. That's all. They didn't d-dig very hard and then they wandered off."

Sorrel thought of boats full of people landing on the coast and chasing Bajacunis to the hills. They would be armed and well equipped – a kind of second coming, unleashing conquest and destruction like in the ancient times she'd read about in the History Module.

Sorrel rose to her feet. "We need to find out for sure what's happening in the rest of the world." She turned to Caroni. "I need the PlAK."

"I've looked already. There's nothing recent."

Sorrel took a deep breath. "I can get into Level 3, maybe even Level 2."

"*What?* Why didn't you say so before?"

"I was afraid – I wanted something to bargain with back then. But it was good here, so I forgot about always looking out. About the world."

"It doesn't matter now," Rashelope said and Sorrel shot her a grateful glance. "Thing is, we have to leave Jiba soon. Where do we go? Are foreigners coming or not? How are they coming? From where?"

Everyone started talking together.

"We just need to find a new p-place to hide," Lichen said, but her small voice was drowned out.

"If people are coming from Amerika, they can land those helicopter troop-carriers and some fighter jets – they don't need boats or runways," Sorrel said. "And they have drones that can blow things up from far away."

"I thought helicopters and airplanes couldn't fly when it got too hot – not enough uplift?" Rashelope said.

"Yes, I remember that," Caroni said. "And the melted runways grounded all the commercial airplanes."

"The Amerikans built huge walls just after the Convergence. And destroyed some of the runways to keep the refugees out, but maybe not all," Sorrel added.

Caroni stood and lifted her hands for quiet. "Sorrel, come with me. Get some rest, people. We'll call you if we find anything useful."

Sorrel sat in front of the PlAK in Caroni's hut. It had been a long while since she sat in front of a screen and her fingers were slow on the keyboard. She logged into Level 4 first, into her old message boards and chatrooms. Her old life. There was a new evacuation order out and revised maps of the Immersion Zone in Bana. The SATMAP showed an irregular coastline with deep inlets reaching into valleys with no towns and cities anymore, as if they had never existed. A map of Bana showed the sea running right through the centre of the city, swallowing what used to be the Ama River. The Barbican Prison, where her father had been held, was gone.

The chatrooms and message boards had hundreds of posts from people trying to find members of their family. The messages had sad headings – Looking for Periwinkle Darliston, last seen at the corner of Azalea and Lily on August 9. My son, Alfred Campbell, drowned in the Ama River July 4. Has anyone seen his body? Then she saw a heading with a single word: One.

She opened the thread, her heart pounding. Hope was too

much like fear. The message said: "One. I hope you see this and you're well and happy. I survived the river. Was captured by the Toplanders. They have everything up here – food, water, houses, solar panels. They blindfolded me, so I don't know how they got me up here. There are many Lowlander captives, slaves, all women. We work on their farms. We're guarded by men with guns. The leader is a vile man called Drax. He made it clear that when I'm no longer useful, they'll throw me off one of the cliffs. They break your legs first. I've seen four Lowlanders thrown off since I've been here so I'm working hard and I'm much stronger. Don't try to find me. I'm risking –" The message ended abruptly. It had been posted almost eight months ago.

"What's wrong?" Caroni said from behind her. Sorrel gestured at the screen; her cheeks wet. "A message from my mother."

Caroni read the post quickly and patted Sorrel's shoulder. "Well, she survived."

"Maybe. She could have died in the last eight months or been killed."

"Let's think about your mother later. You find out what's going on in the rest of the world. Find out if what Lichen heard is true."

It took an hour to hack into Level 2. Not real time, but close. The satellite feeds showed huge plumes of smoke from wildfires sweeping across land and sea in the north. In some pictures, the red of the consuming flames were visible at the base of boiling clouds of smoke. Roads were full of people fleeing on foot. One set of images tracked the massive wall built along Amerika's southern border with Mexitli. It had been breached in several places. Another sequence tracked the wall between Amerika and Kanata. It was mostly intact and heavily patrolled by military vehicles. Amazona had been so thoroughly burned it was a moonscape of black and grey which no longer smouldered. Kanata still had its lakes. There was no ice in Arktikos. The few images of the islands had obviously been taken during a bad dust storm, so Bajacu was hidden.

"We need real time information," Caroni said. Sorrel turned and saw her wiping her eyes. "Can you get into Level 1?"

"I can try. It will take quite a while. Let me stretch my legs." She turned to face Caroni. "It's so *guatan* awful."

"I know." Caroni offered a rare embrace and Sorrel held on to the older woman.

"Tell me when you're ready to start work again."

It was almost dawn before Sorrel broke into Level 1. She went straight to the chat rooms. Lichen had been right. Amerikans were massing on coastlines and there was a plan to evacuate those who could pay to go to various places on ships. There was a list of destinations and Bajacu was one of them.

The PlAK needed charging – its battery was probably on the way out. Her eyes fastened on the last posts and she gave a little gasp. After the Amerikans put out to sea, they would disable their satellites.

That message was ten days old.

CHAPTER 22 – DECIDING

Despite the growing heat, Caroni called everyone to a second band meeting in the shadiest area left. "Stand or sit where I can see you all," Caroni said, looking around. "No one behind me."

They faced their Zorah. "What Lichen heard is true," she began. "The situation in Amerika is terrible and there are huge boats leaving for safer places, mostly islands. Bajacu is one."

"Why islands?" Rashelope said and other girls echoed her question in murmurs. Caroni raised her hand for silence. "Let me tell you everything, and then you can ask your questions. Right. First of all, Sorrel got into Level 1 – real time. I don't have to tell you – this is a *huge* advantage, like having an old-time eye in the sky. And yes, the Northerners are coming. We don't know what they'll do when they get here, but unless they're working with the Domins, there'll be war. I can't see why they'll want to stay on the Lowlands, so, eventually – we don't know how long all of this will take – they'll be up here, looking for higher ground. We don't know what tech they have or what weapons. We don't know how many of them will come. The most important thing, though, is we don't have much time to decide what *we're* going to do, because it seems the Amerikans are going to take their satellites down. Then the world will be truly dark."

"How do you take down a satellite?" Rashelope said. "I thought they stayed in orbit forever, even the ones no one was broadcasting to. Remember there was all that fuss about space junk?"

"I think you boost them into a high orbit where no signals can reach them," Sorrel said, thinking that Bibi would know.

"That's not our focus right now," Caroni said. "You all know we have to leave Jiba at some point, right? There's still some water here, but too little to eat. We must get higher, maybe look for a cave. Somewhere easily defended but close to sources of food. Maybe we even have to split up into two bands." She stopped.

"Are you finished?" Emrallie said.

"Yes."

"Leaving is fine with me. We've been nomads before. We found this place; maybe there are others. We should stay together for now and split if it becomes necessary."

"Sorrel should use Level 1 to look for a good cave," Rashelope said. "If we find one, we go. But I don't think we should just blunder around looking for somewhere better. Jiba still has water and trees for shade – not easy to find. It's defendable too."

"The trees are dying," said Sarane, a quiet eighteen-year-old with curly hair and grey eyes who loved the ravine's trees.

"Dying is not dead," said her friend, Lunar. "And the ravine is still deep in shade."

"Some of us can't walk very well," said Pia. She was a recent arrival and she had a twisted right leg. Lichen had discovered her hiding at the Oconuco dump and had defended her at the ensuing triage discussion.

"If we move too f-far away from B-Bana, we can't scavenge there," Lichen said.

"Maybe there are other towns in the hills," Rashelope said, speaking directly to Lichen. "We've become lazy." Lichen dropped her gaze.

"I'm afraid to leave Jiba," Sarane said. "Maybe the Northerners won't find us; no one else has."

"We might starve on the journey. Starve here, starve in the open. I'd rather starve in Jiba. At least we can fight off ferals here," Emrallie said.

"We can't fight off *anything* if we're starving," Rashelope said.

"We can't travel if we're starving," Sarane countered.

"Caroni?" Sorrel spoke for the first time. "My mother always told me to make a plan. Let me use Level 1 to look for a good place, hopefully within a few days walk. I could look for other towns too. Check out the army camp at Cibao as well – it's really high."

"The PlAK needs charging, you said?"

"Yes."

"How long?"

"It's old now. Could be two, three hours."

"Next time you boot it up, the satellites could be down, right?"

"Maybe. But not all of them. Not at one time."

"I don't see why we need to worry about the satellites – we didn't have a working PlAK for a long time," Rashelope said. "We managed."

"We should avoid that c-camp," stammered Lichen. "I've heard terrible things about it." No one asked her where she got her information.

"Does anyone have anything else to say?" Caroni asked. The lines on her forehead seemed to have grown deeper overnight. No one responded.

"Okay. I've heard you all. I'll decide nextnight about leaving Jiba. Sorrel, charge the PlAK. Then, do some more research. Look for places to shelter and sources of food. Get some rest, people. And no more discussion until Sorrel has done her work."

Nextnight came quickly. Sorrel had tried to sleep, but only managed short, fitful naps as the heat of the day rose and then fell. When she booted up the PlAK at dusk, at least three of the satellites she used regularly were gone and signals were weak and intermittent. She scanned the hills. It was hard to see caves from above, because likely places such as cliffs were often in deep shadow. She spent some time looking at the army camp, but there was a lot of haze and she couldn't see it clearly. There were small figures moving about at the El Dorado cable car – the males were back. And Bana: what was not underwater looked pulverized. Crushed. No retreat, then.

An hour after dusk, Caroni came into the hut Sorrel had so briefly shared with Bibi, and then with Emrallie for almost a year. The Zorah sat beside her. "What did you find?"

"The Northerners won't stay in Bana. There's nothing left. They might land there, but they'll leave as soon as they can. They'll do just what we did – look for a way to get up high. In fact, they've probably already done that."

"Did you find a cave?"

"Not that easy to see from above. But if we follow the river and climb up here –" she pointed – "I think there's a good chance of caves along this stretch of the cliff. I can't tell you about food, though."

"The army camp?"

"Too hazy. A wall right around, though. And we know the Toplanders are dangerous."

"What else?"

"Closest small town is here, in the next valley over, quite far down and it looks really small. Will be difficult to get down and back, assuming we find a cave in the cliff I showed you. But I think there's a small dump on the outskirts that maybe no one has found yet – see? This even looks like a plastic water tank."

"You're right. Maybe there's food in that valley too."

Sorrel moved the cursor and the world the satellite saw, spun and pixelated. "I was just about to look at the bigger picture."

Caroni sat quietly as Sorrel trolled the satellites she could find; she knew them by name: Andromeda, Vega, Aldebaran, and the servers: Range, Fabros, Switch, EnGen, skimming over the ocean with the eyes of a drone, the sea still dotted with the rusting, buckled oil rigs of the fossil-fuel centuries. Finally, she found a town on the blue water of the Ocean of Atlantis, close enough to Bajacu to make an evacuation feasible. No name was given, but it sat where a wide, curving river valley had once met the new edge of the sea. She zoomed in.

The buildings of the town were floating. "That's how they survived," she said to Caroni. "They built houseboats and shopboats."

"The buildings rose with the sea," Caroni agreed. "Place looks military, all those camouflage colours."

Then they both saw the evacuation boats, big ones, many-storeyed. Military vehicles on land, perhaps to keep order. Lines of people. How would such vessels be provisioned? Surely there was not that much food in all the world. How were they powered? How long would the journey take? How would they dock? Or would the Northerners simply moor the boats to the island and live aboard? One vessel had what looked like a small helicopter on deck. They all had lifeboats. Were those respirators on the faces of the people in the lines?

Sorrel panned west and saw the smoke of the fires. If the wind had been in a different direction, she wouldn't have seen the town. On a whim, she changed satellites to look at the Ocean of Atlantis. The screen froze and for a few minutes showed only a few clouds over the vast, crinkled sea. Then, just off the coast of Africa, Sorrel saw a broad swathe of dust in the shape of a teardrop. "Look. A dust storm, coming our way," she said. "When it gets here, we won't be able to travel."

"How many days?"

"I don't know for sure. Depends on the wind. Maybe three or four."

CHAPTER 23 – LEAVING JIBA

Two days later, their possessions were all in tattered bags or tied to their bodies. They broke up the huts and scattered the pieces. They filled in the waste trenches and hid the pathways with fallen leaves and dirt. Every girl was covered with equipment and supplies tied anywhere that string or rope would hold. Every algaskin was full. The tiny breadfruit had been boiled until they dissolved, and they had shared the sticky, tasteless paste. Sorrel could still feel it in her mouth despite hourly rinsing. Water would soon be rationed in sips. Rashelope had an old net in her stores and they stretched it across the dying river and ate the raw fish it caught. Then they ate the tiny river snails, shells and all, and the shrimp they found under the few rocks that were still sitting in water. They caught dragonflies and crickets in smaller nets, roasted them in little underground fires and ate them too. They trapped and ate the few remaining birds – breaking all the rules about the circumstances in which animals could be eaten. Rashelope caught a hummingbird and shared it with no one. They spat out feathers, bones and grit. Some vomited and Sorrel saw the way Caroni looked at them. A dehydrated human was as good as dead.

They had made piles of the things they had accumulated and sorted them over and over again, trying to decide what to abandon and what to take. How heavy was this? How useful was that? They helped each other to find ways to secure their possessions to their bodies. They inspected their shoes and tested them, turning their ankles and pulling at makeshift laces. Sorrel's boots were showing signs of wear. The skins of rodents that had been used to make footwear were patched and repaired.

They didn't know what to do with the large piles of bedding.

Some wanted them burned, others suggested throwing them in the river. Caroni said, no – the fires would be seen, and the river would be blocked.

"Why do we care?" Rashelope demanded. "We're leaving. Who cares what happens to the river?"

Caroni looked at her. "We are not scorched earth people," she said. "If the river is blocked, it will flood and spread out and be seen from the sky."

They packed stores of food – alganola, dried insects, fruit. Very few skynuts.

In the end, they took what they could not carry, hide or destroy to the cave, leaving it far from the entrance, where the roof almost touched the floor.

They planned to leave at dusk. Caroni had told them about the invasion of the Northerners, the big ships, the cliff where there could be caves, and the coming dust storm. No one challenged her decision.

During that last day under the dying trees, they had sat in small groups and no one spoke. Some stretched out on the ground and tried to sleep. Others prowled around; making sure everything useful was packed. Some held knives and machetes and slid their fingers along the blades, honing them on stones if they were not sharp enough. Some walked back and forth to the river, drinking, stripping, lying in the deepest parts. They came back muddy.

Sorrel sat against the trunk of one of the largest trees and wished she knew its name. Its trunk was patterned like an animal's skin; its bark flaked off easily and oozed an orange sap, which they had sometimes used as glue. It dried hard as metal. The tree's leaves were dark green and tiny. Strange dried growths grew on the highest branches. She knew nothing about the tree – not its name, not its uses, not where it came from, or if it belonged in the hills.

She thought about Emrallie's words: *I don't think about humanity*. She suddenly understood Emrallie's rejection of the old people and their old ways.

But we're the same, she thought. Once the band had stopped moving and arrived at Jiba, we started wanting, gathering and keeping more. Any kind of thin, dirty bedding had been luxurious when we first arrived at camp. I saw others with more and wanted more for myself. If we'd been able to stay here, we would've used it all up, too.

The morning before they left, they heard a rumbling noise and the earth shook. The trees rustled and all the girls who were standing dropped to their hands and knees. They were used to earthquakes, but this one seemed to go on for a long time. The land rocked like the ocean, all crest and trough. Sorrel was hot under all the things tied to her and her hair was wet under her hat. She suddenly wanted her hair to be gone. This part of her life was over.

The earthquake stopped and she took out the old razor, which had been charged along with everything that could be charged. She had kept it because it reminded her of Bibi, and the day they had shaved each other's bodies. She took off her hat and began to shave her head.

The others watched as her hair fell in long curls. When she had finished, they came over, one by one, and took the razor. They formed a line, and the Tribals shaved their heads until the razor ran out of charge. The pile of hair grew. Rashelope pulled a cloth bag from her backpack and stuffed it full. No one asked her why.

"I'll put the razor back on charge. It'll only take a couple hours," Sorrel said to her.

"I'll keep my hair," Rashelope said.

That afternoon, it began to rain, a steady, cooling old-time rain. The remaining trees broke the force of the water, and it fell on them in fat drops. Water coursed down tree trunks and into the earth, which began to release a loamy, wet smell. There was no wind. "Will we still leave at dusk?" asked Lichen, her voice trembling.

"Yes, that's what I'd thought," Caroni said. "Rain is a good friend to us." She shook her head and stood. "But there's no need to wait. We go now."

They rose to their feet together and Rashelope led them in single file to the river. She had her machete and rusty shovel strapped to her back in the shape of an X. It was hard to see in the rain and no one spoke. Their journey would get harder as it got dark, but the ravine, now with just a small stream, offered an easy path. The river had fallen at least a metre from the last time Sorrel had seen it. They were safe when the river was a torrent, because they were hidden under the tree canopy. Now that it was drying up and the leaves were falling, they'd soon have been found. She strode past Landis and Genus, who were relative newcomers to the band. She knew little about them.

She fell in behind Rashelope and Emrallie. She was strong now but knew how quickly her fitness would ebb if they didn't find food. Lichen walked up beside her and she touched the younger girl's shoulder. They walked on in the rain, leaving Jiba behind.

It rained all night and through the next day. Caroni said there would be no rest and no drinking from the algaskins. "Drink from the sky," she said.

"I don't like this rain," Sorrel whispered to Emrallie.

"Why not? What's the matter with you?"

"It's not normal."

Emrallie laughed. "What's normal?"

"How many times have you seen rain like this?"

"Maybe never. But so what? It's just rain. What's the worst that can happen – a rain bomb? A hurricane? Another earthquake? We'll find a place to hide –" She stopped abruptly. "You're just spooked by leaving camp."

"Maybe. I don't know if we'll find a cave today. What if it stops raining soon and we're still outside?"

"Just walk. Be glad you can walk. Be glad the going is pretty easy. Be glad we're together. Be glad we ate something yesterday. Stop thinking."

"That breadfruit paste was disgusting."

"It was just fuel."

"Yeah, but I remember the breadfruit we got on our first night in camp. Now that was *food.*"

"*Guata*, Sorrel, you're always looking back." Emrallie lengthened her stride and left her.

The rain started to ease at 1500 hours. "Three hours to dusk," Caroni said, taking off her hat. She looked strange without hair.

"It's going to heat up quickly. Spread out, people. Look for shelter. Any kind of shelter, but a cave would be best. Leave your packs here. Lichen, you stay with the stuff."

Sorrel shed her backpack, but instead of feeling unburdened she felt more vulnerable. They were still in the ravine, but it had narrowed, and they were on a path closer to the top of the cliffs she had seen on the PlAK, the riverbed now twenty metres below. Maybe there *would* be caves. Then she thought about being deep underground, and not knowing whether the rain had restarted, had turned into a rain bomb, and the river was rising. Or whether rocks would crash onto them in an earthquake.

She could see a faint waterline on the rocks far above her head and fault lines cutting through the cliffs. It might be best to rest for just a few hours until it was dark and then walk again through nextnight, but what would Caroni do if one of them couldn't go on?

She rounded a slight curve and found herself behind two huge rocks. No one could see her, and she was glad to be alone for a moment. She sat in the shadow of one of the rocks, remembering the night with Bibi in the tree root cavern just after they left Bana, and her childhood hiding place under the rock that had burned her cheek. Her mother was her only living relative – assuming she was still alive. She had Bibi's oval toes and straight eyebrows, her father's downturned mouth. They lived in her. She touched the scar on her cheek and shook off her thoughts. Maybe Emrallie was right – she spent too much time in the past.

She was thirsty but too tired to hike down to the river. She disobeyed Caroni's instructions and took two sips from her algaskin and the small resistance cheered her. She didn't understand the Zorah's decision to stop now. Night was coming, and they should keep moving, especially because they were still in the ravine and the direct rays of the sun only reached the bottom in certain places.

She heard the rattle of dislodged stones and jumped to her feet. She scanned the cliff face and saw a substantial ledge about five metres above her head which seemed to lead to a steep path at one end. The path snaked up the cliff and disappeared behind an overhang. She listened, but there were no more sounds, except the dripping of water left behind by the rain.

"See anything?" Emrallie said, arriving. She had kept her backpack.

"No. Maybe. See that ledge?" She pointed. "A little to the right. Did you kick loose some stones?"

"No, I don't think so."

"I heard something."

"What?"

"Maybe nothing. Do you see the ledge?"

"I see a ledge. So what? Couldn't even hold four of us."

"Look at the south end. There's a path…"

"Okay, I see a path. And?"

"Well, the path goes behind that overhang and doesn't come out again. Why would there be a path that doesn't go all the way to the top? Or come down to where the river was?"

Emrallie grunted. "What're you thinking?"

"Maybe it goes into a cave that we can't see because the entrance is behind the overhang."

"Huh. It's possible." Emrallie shrugged her pack off her shoulders. "One way to find out."

"No, wait, Em, let's wait for the others. It's such a long shot. And anyway, how're you going to even get to the ledge?"

"Watch me." She untied the rope she always wore around her waist and gave the end to Sorrel. She checked her knots and sank her palms into a patch of sand to improve her grip. "Five metres. Nothing."

"Wait, Em, suppose…" Sorrel had not finished speaking before Emrallie was off the ground. She hung onto a narrow rock ledge with her fingers, her feet planted flat against the rock face, legs almost straight, moving sideways like the crabs that used to live on Bana's waterfront, inching higher with every step. One of her footholds gave way and she hung from her arms for a few seconds. "*Guata!*" she yelled. She found another foothold and kept climbing.

In less than five minutes she was sitting on the ledge. "Told ya!" she shouted. "I'm gonna find a place to tie the rope, in case I have to come down in a hurry. Then see what there is to see."

Rashelope came up. "What's happening? What's all the shouting about?"

Sorrel pointed. "Emrallie is checking out that path – maybe it ends in a cave."

"How'd she get up there?"

"She climbed."

Rashelope whistled in admiration. "Even if there's a cave, we'll never get everybody up there."

"She took a rope up with her." Sorrel showed her the end of rope she still held.

"Smart."

They stood watching Emrallie's small figure as she began to climb the path. She progressed in bouncy, effortless strides, holding on a few times with her hands. Then she disappeared behind the overhang.

"If she comes back right away, there's nothing there," Rashelope said.

Sorrel murmured her agreement. Slowly the other members of the band joined them on the narrow path. They were all panting like canines and bathed in sweat. The sun was just beginning its retreat up the cliffs. "It's Emrallie," they whispered to each other. "She climbed up there."

"I can't do that," Lichen said.

Then they heard Emrallie whoop again from behind the overhang. "There *is* a cave," she yelled. "And it's huge. And I think it'll take us out of here!"

"Come down, Emrallie," Caroni shouted.

"Not yet. Send Rashelope up with more rope! We can tie the rope onto rocks the whole way up. I dunno, maybe we can even stay here. It's underground, but high. And the walls drip, so there's water."

"Wait. Where does the path we're on lead to, Sorrel?" Caroni asked. "Around the corner."

"I didn't look. I was just taking a break when I saw it."

"Go and look now."

The path curved around the mountain and became steadily narrower, until it stopped at a circular breakaway. Sorrel swayed on her feet and put her hand on the cliff at her left to steady herself. She was the wrong person to explore a narrow, precipitous path and she felt angry with Caroni. *Look up*, she thought.

The cliff above her head was sheer – she could see no way up. Then a slice of rock flaked away her under her hand and shattered at her feet. The geology had changed – these rocks wouldn't hold the ropes or their weight. She pressed her back to the rock face and turned slowly to retrace her steps, wanting to flee, but forcing herself to test every footstep before transferring her weight.

"Well?" Caroni said when she returned.

"We don't have a choice. The path ends in a breakaway not far away and it's treacherous. And the cliff's made of a different kind of rock, breaks up in your hand."

"That's it, then," Caroni said.

Rashelope wrapped herself in rope until she looked like an old-time turtle. She used the first stretch Emrallie had already secured to climb up to the ledge and then they began cutting handholds into the path to the overhang, looping the rope around crags and outcroppings. Even looking up made Sorrel's head swim.

By the time the ropes were fixed, it was dusk. "Lichen!" Rashelope shouted. "You come up first. You can do it!"

The Zorah stepped forward, her hand on Lichen's elbow. "We'll go together," she said to the girl. "I'll be right behind you. Sorrel, you bring up the rear – make sure everyone is up before you leave."

Despite what she'd said earlier, Lichen didn't hesitate. Her eyes shone with unshed tears and her small hands trembled, but she grasped the rope and began climbing, hesitating at every step. Sorrel wanted to bawl at her to get on with it. The sense of vulnerability and threat she had felt since leaving Jiba was growing.

She heard the rattle of dislodged stones again. "Did you hear that?" she said to Caroni, who had just begun her climb behind Lichen. The Zorah stopped half a metre off the ground.

"Hear what?"

"Stones falling. I think someone – something is coming."

"Take two of the girls and stay at the rear. Keep a good watch."

They jostled each other as Caroni gained height, all desperate now to be off the ground.

"Come with me," Sorrel said to Genus and Landis, who were

closest to her, both with the handles of old-time tools strapped to their backs. Just as they pushed their way through the remaining group a pack of ferals charged towards them. At least eight porcs. The two in front were huge, the one to the right had a broken tusk.

"Don't let them get past!" she screamed to Genus and Landis. "Caroni, go faster! Get everyone up!"

The Zorah's voice came from above. "Climb, people! Hurry. Look for somewhere on the path to shelter. Get off the rope if you can, to let others climb." Sorrel knew there was nowhere on the path to shelter. She faced the feral pack, which came to a halt about two metres away.

The narrow path stopped the porcs from surrounding the three girls, but also limited their ability to swing their weapons without hitting each other. Sorrel was the only one with a good blade and she stepped in front of the other two, machete in hand. "They'll try to knock you off your feet with their tusks," she cried to the others, without looking around. "Use their momentum to hit them off the path!"

The two big porcs in front held their heads low, the others crowding behind. Their smell filled her with revulsion. *Wait*, she told herself. *Let them come to you.* She heard the sounds of the group climbing behind her, but she feared they were not going fast enough. She stared at a spot behind the biggest porc's ear until she could see nothing else.

The big porc rushed her, swinging its massive tusks at her legs. She screamed and swung the machete at its neck and felt the blade bite. Blood spattered her face. The shock of connecting with the huge animal travelled up her arm and she almost dropped her weapon. The animal squealed and fell, its body sprawled across the path. She whirled to meet the second porc's attack and felt its single tusk rip through her pants, just slicing her leg. She jumped back, colliding with Genus and leaving Landis slightly in front. The porc charged at Landis and the girl slipped and lost her footing. The feral skewered her in the groin, wrenching its head from side to side, snarling, ripping her open. It began tearing at her face. Sorrel leapt at the animal, slid her machete under its neck and slit its throat. She felt the porc's rough, stinking skin against her own and she could not bear being so close to it. She rolled off into the pumping blood on the path. She heard Genus's long wail of terror from behind her.

She leapt up, facing the feral pack. Six more to fight. The two dead porcs lay on the trail next to Landis's faceless body. Her arm felt leaden and her leg was on fire. Then a feral trotted forward to bite at one of the porc carcasses. Another one ripped at Landis's clothes and then the pack began to tear animal and human apart. She shuddered.

"Now, Sorrel!" Emrallie yelled from above. "They're distracted!"

"Go!" she said to Genus. "Run! *Guatan* do what I tell you!" She pushed her hard and the girl ran, still sobbing.

"I don't want to turn my back on them," she shouted to Emrallie. The light was failing and she could not see her friend.

"I'm going to bring down some rocks to block the path. I'm not going to leave you here."

The smell of the feral pack came in waves and she heard the sound of flesh ripping. Her gorge rose. "I'm ready now, Sorrel," Emrallie shouted. "*Guatan* run!"

Sorrel turned on her heel and ran along the path towards the ropes. She caught a glimpse of Emrallie on the cliff above, her legs braced against a pile of rocks. She pushed and they came down in a landslide, a rock hitting Sorrel's shoulder a glancing blow. "Don't look behind," Emrallie cried. "The ropes are there. Just climb. I have your back."

CHAPTER 24 – HIGH CAVE

It was almost night and the cave Emrallie had found held a denser blackness inside. Sorrel stood at the entrance and waited for her friend. Caroni was consoling Genus, whose shoulders still shook, and the girls gathered around them, many of them crying.

Landis's body had been left for the porcs.

Sorrel retched, but nothing came up. "Drink some water," Caroni said, over Genus's shoulder. Lichen left the group and came to stand by Sorrel. "Y-you did your best," she said. "No one could have done more."

Maybe I could have, Sorrel thought. *You weren't there to see*. She thought she might faint. She was filthy, covered in blood. She remembered the first time she saw the river and what it felt like to lie in it, the water rushing past.

Emrallie came over the ledge and Sorrel saw that she was exhausted. She tripped at the smallest of ridges at the cave's entrance and sprawled on the ground. She lay without moving. "Em? Are you okay?" Sorrel said, squatting beside her. She offered an algaskin. Emrallie didn't respond but she drank.

"Are either of you hurt?" Caroni said.

"No but I hate those *guatan* things," Emrallie said from the ground. "*Guatan* hate them. We have to find a place they can't get to. I want to go back to eating them."

Sorrel looked at her ripped pants. "A little," she said to Caroni. Her thigh was beginning to throb.

"Let me look," Caroni said, bending over to look. "Hmm. Just a cut. Not deep. If it doesn't get infected, you'll be fine. I think I have a little rum in my pack. I'll get it."

She returned with a small glass bottle. "You fought well. Both of you. I'm sorry about Landis, but…" Her voice trailed off.

"This'll burn. Hold still." She poured careful drops of rum on Sorrel's cut. "Keep it clean," she said. Then she held out her hand to Emrallie and pulled her to her feet. "Come farther inside. We'll set guards."

They followed Caroni to the back of the cave. Sorrel wanted to lean against Emrallie but she squared her shoulders and resisted the impulse, which she knew would be unwelcome.

They lay around like fallen branches, their heads on their packs or piles of extra clothes, their eyes swollen from crying. Rashelope rested dry-eyed, her head on the bag of hair. The torches flared straight up into the heavy, motionless air. They couldn't see the roof of the cave, but sensed it was large. No one spoke of Landis. Sorrel smelled of porc and blood and the cut on her thigh was on fire.

Emrallie knelt beside her. "Here," she said, handing her a wet rag. "Clean yourself up."

She wiped her face and hands and lay down. The floor of the cave was hard but smooth, and she remembered that the whole ravine had once been underground. If water had carved this cave, it might be part of a series of subterranean channels, which could now be pathways, leading them out of the ravine. But leading them where?

Sorrel lay in the dark, listening to Emrallie's breathing beside her. Would she ever stop reliving Landis's death? Think of Jiba, she told herself. She had worked in the garden every afternoon and had loved tending the stony soil, watching the insects come, the flowers appearing, the reaping of the food. She tried to hold their lives at Jiba in her mind, but all she could see was Landis's mutilated body. She knew nothing of Landis's life story. No one who had been part of her history would know of her dying. She groaned in the dark and Emrallie reached out and touched her bare head. "It's better she died."

"How can you *say* that?"

"Suppose she had lived with a serious injury? Suppose we had to care for her during a long dying? Sleep. We're safe here. For now."

Daylight came. The Tribals stirred. The back of the cave was still in darkness, but they could see the sides nearest to the entrance where Rashelope sat with one of the torches. Had she been on guard all night?

"We should look for signs of animals using this cave and get the dead porcs," Emrallie said, sitting up and looking around. "*Guatan* eat them." She sounded more like herself. She stood slowly. "Ow. Everything hurts."

Caroni came over to them. "They'll have started to rot already. Porcs have diseases. We can't afford anyone getting sick. Take out the PlAK, Sorrel. Let's have a good look at this cave."

She shone the searchlight at the high roof. It was smooth and rounded, as the floor was, and fissured in many places. In the bright light the rocks were pale grey, and there were lines of slowly dripping water gathering along the cracks.

"Well, there's water," Caroni said.

Sorrel followed the curving walls with the searchlight and found two openings at the back. "Should we explore?" she said.

"Yes, but later. We have to use string to make sure we can find our way back. Let's relieve Rashelope and eat something. Go and check on Genus."

Sorrel shook her head. She couldn't face Genus yet. "I want to see what kind of signal there is. I'll get Rashelope and stay at the entrance." She didn't wait for the Zorah's approval.

"Keep the torch burning," Rashelope said, handing it to Sorrel. "It's for the ferals."

You really don't have to tell me that, she thought. Rashelope's eyes were red-rimmed and puffy. She moved stiffly back into the cave.

Sorrel looked out. She could feel the rising heat from the floor of the ravine far below and although it was early, the light was blinding. She put on her dark glasses. She saw the ropes Emrallie had set and the path where she had fought the porcs. It was strewn with lumps of flesh and bone and it was impossible to separate animal from human. She closed her eyes. She didn't know what was above them or where the openings at the back of the cave led to, but only avian ferals could reach them from the front. She extinguished the torch in the gravel at her feet. She heard low talk behind her and was glad to be alone.

She booted up the PlAK. One more satellite gone. The direction finder located them under a craggy mountain. No one could climb down to them unless they could rappel. No animals could get to them from above. She began to feel better about the cave. Cool, even in the day. Water available. Easily defended. Now to find food.

She zoomed out, looking for green patches and water. High up, the tiny flash of a spring wound its way through feathery bamboo groves, and she followed it downstream to the army camp called Cibao, maybe a day's walk away. It was where Bibi had said she was held by Toplanders.

Caroni came up and looked at the PlAK's screen over her shoulder. "There's a signal?"

"Yes, but one more satellite has gone," Sorrel said. "That's where my mother was. Is." She pointed to the roofs of the army camp. They were peaked, so there were no succulents planted. Many had solar panels. The camp looked cared for. Organized.

"Was," Caroni said.

"No one ever wants to talk about her."

"What's the point?"

Sorrel turned to the PlAK and Caroni watched the images stutter and pixelate.

"Are we going to stay here then?" Sorrel said, waiting for the frozen screen to resolve.

"Depends what's nearby and where those openings at the back lead. There's shelter and water. Looks like the front can be defended. I can't see how a feral can get up here."

Sorrel nodded, thinking about Toplanders and Northerners. "Maybe we should take down the ropes?"

"Yes. But not before we find another way down. And food. Anything growing."

"What about earthquakes?"

"We can't worry about earthquakes."

Caroni gathered the band together near to the entrance. Sorrel half listened to her instructions. They were to eat and drink sparingly. Calabash bowls were to be set under the dripping water. Bodily functions were to be done outside – Genus and Sarane were to look for a good place and excavate a trench, if possible.

"I don't want to go outside," Genus said.

Caroni ignored her. "Make sure the trench is downwind of the cave entrance, but not far away. Take Rashelope's shovel – "

"I'm keeping my shovel," Rashelope said.

"Here, use mine," Lunar said. "I'll go with you."

"Everyone, split into two groups and explore those openings with the torches. Take string and unroll it. Mark the walls as well. Stop when the string runs out. Look for light."

"Why hasn't someone already found this cave?" Emrallie said.

"It was all underwater, remember. Sorrel, you go with Lichen into one of the exits."

"I want to stay and use the PlAK," Sorrel said. "It's day outside – it can be charged easily."

There was a long moment before Caroni replied and Sorrel sensed that after the mention of Bibi, the Zorah was still assessing her trustworthiness – after almost a year. She glared at the Zorah. "You want to do the looking?"

Caroni didn't respond right away. Then her gaze softened. "Look for food," she said. "And yes, check out the army camp too. You'll tell us *everything*."

At dusk, they gathered for a meeting. The torches were lit, and the girls stared into the flames. The string had run out before an exit had been found.

"There are many different t-tunnels. It would be easy t-to get lost," Lichen said, sounding defensive.

"Why didn't you just follow the marks you cut?" Caroni snapped.

"The walls are very crumbly. We couldn't find some of our own marks. It would be better if we had a piece of coal, something like that. Plus, you said stop when the string ran out."

"Sorrel, what can you tell us? What about food?"

"The camp is the nearest thing to us, but it's heavily defended. Wall right around. There was a lot of haze and the signal was poor, so I couldn't see any people clearly. I thought I could see the valley and the small town we saw in Jiba, same coordinates, but it looked different, I don't know why. It's a good three days away and far below us. I don't know if it's practical for foraging."

"No food near, then?"

"Not that I could see. Not today, anyway, visibility too poor. We're under a big rocky mountain. Maybe tomorrow will be clearer."

"Probably another satellite down tomorrow. We need to hunt ferals," Rashelope said. "Set traps. Cooking will kill the germs."

No one answered.

"I think we should stay here," Genus said. "The foragers should go out and find food."

"Easy to say," Rashelope said.

"From now on, we ration our food and share it equally," Caroni said. "Bring your food to me. Every piece of it."

"Bigger, stronger people should get more," Rashelope said, glaring at Lichen and Genus.

"You can leave that to me," the Zorah said.

CHAPTER 25 – MALES

Six days later, they were still in the cave. Each day, Caroni had sent a different group of girls to search for food, and each day, they came back empty handed. The traps they set for small birds or rodents were unsprung. "There's nothing nearby," Rashelope said, getting angrier with each attempt. "We have to stay out overday, like we used to in Jiba. We need to range much farther."

"You said there were many signs of ferals. If we're travelling, we travel together," Caroni said.

Other girls had explored the tunnels as far as they dared and found no sign of an exit.

Conditions had remained hazy and there was little to see from the remaining satellites. "Maybe we should make for that valley and the small town we saw?" Emrallie said. "Where is it?"

Sorrel shrugged and gestured at the screen. "Can't see much. Been like that since we got here."

Caroni spent much of her time at the front of the cave looking out, her brow creased with worry. For the first time since encountering the Tribals, Sorrel felt that they were leaderless.

On the seventh afternoon, it started to rain in strange, short bursts. She went to the front of the cave. "This should clear the haze," she said to the Zorah.

"Yes. It might."

"Can we stand in the rain, Caroni? We're all filthy and demoralized. Starving too. If we don't find food soon, we won't be able to travel anywhere."

"I know. Yes, but strip. Keep your clothes dry. Go in groups. Come inside if it gets too heavy."

Sorrel stood outside with Emrallie, Genus and Lichen. They were all naked and every rib was visible. Their pelvises looked scooped out. They turned their faces upwards to the pulses of rain and did not look at each other. "You've had enough," Rashelope said from the cave. "Time for someone else. The rain might stop anytime."

Being washed clean by the rain improved morale and afterwards, they sat around, eating the small amounts of food shared out by Caroni – alganola, two dried insects each, one piece of dried fruit. They had drunk so much their stomachs felt full. "Tomorrow we'll send a group to the camp at dusk," Caroni said. "Another group will try to find the valley with the town, if Sorrel can find it on the PlAK. And we must find the end of the tunnels."

Next morning, Caroni sent girls to explore the tunnels, led by Emrallie. "Go to the end of one tunnel at a time," she said. "Spread out, but don't lose sight of each other. Rashelope, you take a group to the army camp as soon as it's cool enough. See what's possible there, even if just to steal some food. I'll take a third group to see if we can find the valley town we saw. We'll take double rations."

"At night?" Sorrel said.

"Just give us a direction. I have a compass. We don't have a choice. We'll die here if we don't find food. You'll stay and keep using the PlAK. I'm going to leave the band's food with you. Ration it carefully."

"I won't be able to see anything from the satellites at night."

"No, but you can still visit chat rooms. We need information. Maybe we have to go down instead of up. Or into the middle of the island. Look for news of the dust storm."

Those exploring the tunnels had left. Rashelope was getting ready with her group, sorting possessions, leaving everything unnecessary behind. Caroni's group were resting. For those remaining in the cave, it was going to be a long day of waiting.

Sorrel took the PlAK to the entrance and settled down to her search. The sky was finally clear and, on the screen, Cibao seemed close enough to touch. Rashelope's group walked past her. No one spoke.

She began a methodical search of the mountains in quadrants. A world of rock and cliff. Not a single tree or shrub. Then, just as she was about to move to the middle of the island, she caught a glimpse of a smudge of green, half hidden behind a ridge. She zoomed in close and the screen froze. Don't give up on me now, she whispered to the PlAK. She waited. The image resolved and revealed a round, green valley, like a bowl, with a spring falling into it from the top of a cliff. "A waterfall!" Sorrel cried. "Green. Caroni!"

Together, they looked at the screen. "It's about the same distance as Cibao," Sorrel said, "but as the crow flies. Much more difficult terrain in between. I don't know if we can get there."

"Someone has," Caroni said. The valley held slanted shelters, open on three sides, and there were two tiny standing figures. "I wonder who they are. Those are lean-tos." Then they saw another figure on the ground, braced on its arms. "Push-ups," Caroni said. "Males."

"They found a nice place," Sorrel said.

"Looks like it. But males…" Caroni shook her head.

"Maybe instead of the town, that's where you should go?"

"I don't know…"

A cloud obscured the round valley. "Let me look for the dust storm before I lose visibility." Sorrel panned over the Ocean of Atlantis. She pointed at the plume, now in the shape of a ragged oval. "It'll soon be here," she said. "If we're still in this cave, we won't be able to leave, maybe for days. Then we'll be too weak to travel. We'll starve."

Caroni sighed and rubbed her eyes. "See if you can find a route to the male camp."

Pia, Sarane and Lunar remained in the cave with Sorrel. Except for Pia, they were all older and got tired easily. Pia had an old injury – she'd broken her ankle as a child, and it had not set properly. Sorrel knew none of them well. Even in such a small band, people now spent most of their time in even smaller groups of two or three.

It was late afternoon and the light and heat were ebbing. The PlAK had been charged and Caroni had left with her group for the male camp near the waterfall. Sorrel noticed that she didn't tell them about the change of destination. They were probably too tired and hungry to care.

"What're you hoping to find?" Pia said from across the cave. She sat with her bad leg extended. Sarane and Lunar had gone outside to relieve themselves.

"Nothing. Anything."

"What about earlier? Did you find what you're – what we're – looking for?"

"I think so."

"Bad or good?"

"Information's always good."

"Tell me."

"When everyone gets back," Sorrel said. It had been many hours since the group exploring the cave tunnels had left. She wished Emrallie would return.

Pia's face was strained. "Your foot hurts, huh?" Sorrel asked.

"Every hour of every day. But I can cope with the pain," she added. It was Pia's way of assuring them that she wasn't going to be a burden on the group. Maybe the strain on the older girl's face wasn't pain but fear of abandonment. She remembered Emrallie telling her that Caroni was a good Zorah and would make the right decision. She had let Pia travel with them. Sorrel wanted to comfort her but wasn't sure what to say. If Pia really couldn't walk, she *would* be left behind. She got up to stretch her legs and heard low voices. *Emrallie's group*, she thought, relieved.

Then four young males walked into the cave from one of the tunnels at the rear. They halted, shock on the face of the boy in front. Sorrel reached over her shoulder for her machete and realised she had taken it off. The only weapon she carried was the knife.

"Who the *guata* are you?" she snapped.

"A foul-mouthed female," said the male in front. "And is that a PlAK?" He looked about seventeen.

They were all teenagers. Some were dressed in camouflage gear and all wore good boots. One held a long gun.

"Are you the band in the valley with the waterfall?" she asked, her brain racing.

"Spied on us, did you?" the same boy said, pulling his shoulders back like an army recruit. He was tall and gangly. His arms were bare, and his muscles looked like rope. His dark glasses were pushed up on his forehead. He had unusual light eyes, neither blue nor grey. Behind her, Pia had scrambled to her feet.

"Well, are you?" Sorrel demanded.

"We're in a valley, yes. And you?"

"We're stragglers," she said, trying to buy some time. She gestured at Pia's injury. "We couldn't keep up."

"Stragglers from where? Keep up with who?"

"We lived in the ravine below. The river used to fill it up, but then it started falling and…"

"We? Where're the others?"

"They left us."

The light-eyed male looked sceptical. "I can understand why they'd leave you, but I don't believe anyone would've left the PlAK. Try a different story."

"They didn't know how to use it."

"Everybody can use a PlAK," he scoffed. "We'll be taking it anyway."

Sorrel had never been face-to-face with a group of young

135

males before. The one holding the gun stood back, cradling it with the butt under his arm, the muzzle pointing down. Had he been in the Squad? He scanned the group from right to left and back again. *Coiled to strike*, she thought.

"Females are useful," said one of the other boys, standing just behind the one with the gun. It sounded like something he had learned in school. He was skeletal with straight black hair and he squinted. He probably needed glasses. "They're great at finding food. I saw that somewhere."

"Females can think," Sorrel retorted. "Plan. Cooperate. Work. And in this case, use the PlAK to find out things you can't. What level are you?" She stared at the boy with light eyes.

The males exchanged glances but didn't respond.

Pia limped forward to stand beside to Sorrel. "I'm Pia, and this is Sorrel. What are your names?"

"Flower name," the boy in front said, gazing at Sorrel. He had a groove between his eyebrows which made him look worried. "You're from Bana. I'm – I was – from there too. I'm Kes." He gestured to the others. "Slate, Journey and Rapt."

"Rapt?" Pia said. "Like in –"

"Raptor," the boy with the gun scowled. His voice was scratchy, as if he rarely used it.

Silence fell. No one seemed to know what to do. Four males with one gun. They could take the band's possessions and then throw them all off the cliff. There could be serious injuries if they fought. She saw Landis's split belly in her mind and remembered the old woman she'd seen reduced to a pile of rags in minutes in Bana.

"Let's sit," she said. "Tell us about your band and I'll tell you about ours. I'll show you what I saw on the PlAK. We're no danger to you. Maybe we could help." Should she mention Sarane and Lunar outside? Or the other members of the band in the tunnels who might return at any moment?

Kes looked at the boys with him and raised his hands in a what-do-you-think gesture. The one with the squint – Slate – nodded.

"I don't know," said the male called Journey. He was pale and freckled with a wispy reddish beard.

"At least ask *him* to put down the gun," Sorrel said to Kes, inclining her head in Rapt's direction.

Rapt made a sound of disdain. "I'll wait outside. Under the overhang. Call me when you're ready to do – whatever."

"He doesn't talk much," Slate said. It sounded like an apology.

They stood in an uneven circle and no one spoke at first. Where were Sarane and Lunar? Had they heard the males and hid?

"We're a band of females," Sorrel began, speaking directly to Kes. Before she could go much further, they heard voices and Emrallie walked out of the tunnels into the cave, her group behind her. Her shoulders were slumped, and she stared at the ground in front of her. Sorrel guessed their search hadn't been successful.

Emrallie stopped short when she saw the males. She dropped her torch and reached for her machete. "It's okay," Sorrel said, lifting her hands, palms out. Some of the girls stepped back into the relative darkness of the tunnel. "Come in," she said. "We're talking."

"Who are you?" Emrallie demanded.

"There's a valley nearby," Sorrel explained. "Zorah and I spotted it when the cloud cleared. These males live there – Kes, Slate, Journey and Rapt is outside. We were just beginning to talk. Shall we all sit?"

"I'll stand. Who are you?" Emrallie asked again.

"Maybe you could put down the machete," Kes said.

"Rapt still has his gun," Sorrel snapped.

"Someone has a *gun*?" Emrallie said.

The encounter was spiralling out of control. "Let's just listen for a minute," Sorrel said to Emrallie as more of the girls walked into the cave from the tunnels.

"We're a band of twenty-three," Kes began, "and we've been in the valley for about six years." There was a waterfall, he told them, which was their source of water. It was the reason they'd settled there, but it was declining now. They'd found fruit trees nearby, but they'd stopped bearing. At the bottom of the waterfall there was a pool with fish and shrimp and snails, very few now, but it flowed a short distance over land before it disappeared underground.

"We used to be able to trap birds and catch insects, but they're all gone," he said, looking at his hands.

"Where'd you get the military gear?" Emrallie asked.

"Raids on the army camp, before the wall had been built. The Toplanders have been there for a long time, but at first there weren't many of them and I guess they weren't expecting raids. They had a different leader then. We've tried a few times, but they're waiting for you as soon as you come over the wall, even at night. We lost two like that. Alba was killed outright, and Llando was captured. They cut off Llandos's head and drop-kicked it over the wall." Kes stopped. "We don't know what happened to their bodies."

There was silence.

"The camp has a different stream?" Sorrel asked.

"They have water – could be the same river, different tributary, I don't know."

"Did you see any slaves, the time you attacked?"

"I didn't see anything, but the guns aimed at me and two dead friends," Kes said. "But I've heard there are slaves, yes."

"The Toplanders have military training?" Emrallie asked.

"Some do, for sure. We think their ammunition could be running low."

"Why d'you think that?" Sorrel said.

"Our valley has a good view of the best approach to the camp. There's nothing going in. But maybe it's wishful thinking – we don't know how much they started with. And people could be moving at night."

"What else do you know about the Toplanders?"

"Only what everyone knows. Elites. Slavers. Led by a man called Colonel Drax. I'm sure you've heard about him. Toplanders are vicious."

All the girls were now in the cave, most of them sitting and listening intently to Kes. "Your turn," he said to Sorrel. "Are you the band leader?"

How much should she tell him? "We lived in the ravine until the river started falling," she said. "We ran out of food."

"You didn't answer my question. Are you the leader? How many of you?"

"There're two more groups outside. Seventeen – no, sixteen."

"You're not sure?"

"One died getting up here. Ferals."

"Are you the leader?"

"No. She's outside."

"What were you looking for in the tunnels?" Pia interrupted, speaking to Kes.

"Today, you mean?"

"Yes."

"We knew the river was falling. We used to hear it rushing, but we couldn't get down to it. Then it got quieter and quieter. Arc – *our* leader – sent us to try again; maybe there was a place we could live at the bottom. Time spent in recce is never wasted."

"Recce?"

"Reconnaissance. Arc is – was – a Domin brat."

"We couldn't find an exit," Emrallie said, staring at Kes. "I don't believe your story."

"The exit would be very hard to find from this end – the access is narrow and between two slanted slabs of rock. You'd have to be looking directly at it. We found a sinkhole close to our camp and it had the remains of a rusty ladder, too broken up to use, but we knew it must have led somewhere. From the other side, the path leads straight to the opening."

"Can you find it again? This sinkhole?" Pia asked.

Kes rolled his eyes. "Of course. Our band is guarding it and there's a rope. Like I said, it's not far."

Then they heard the sound of a scuffle at the entrance, a short scream, quickly cut off, and Rapt walked in, pushing Lunar in front of him. A bruise bloomed on her cheek.

"We're wasting time," he rasped to Kes. "We should take the PlAK and go. Decide what to do with them." He nodded at the circle of girls. "There's another one outside. I knocked her out. She'll be okay," he added, watching Kes's face. He pushed Lunar forward and she fell to her knees.

"You *guatan* hit her?" Sorrel said, jumping to her feet, hand on the knife at her waist. "For *what*?" Emrallie took a step towards Rapt and he lifted the gun to his shoulder. Everyone froze.

"You okay, Lunar?" Sorrel said.

"Yeah, I guess. I don't know about Sarane, though. That one," she nodded at Rapt, "he hit her with the gun. We tried to hide when we heard them, but there just wasn't anywhere, it's all rock and – " She began crying.

"*Guatan* males," Sorrel hissed. "My mother warned me about you."

A voice outside the cave said, "What happened? Did you fall?"

Rashelope! Sorrel could not make out Sarane's reply, but Rashelope said, "Wait here." She came into the cave holding her shovel. Emrallie joined her, machete in hand, and they stood, shoulder to shoulder, facing the four males.

"Who are you?" Rashelope said. "And why the *guata* is Sarane bleeding?"

"He *guatan* hit her," Sorrel said, pointing at Rapt. "He hit Lunar too. They were outside and –"

"They're planning to take the PlAK and hurt us," Pia said.

"They're the band we saw in the valley. They know about the army camp. We should –" Sorrel said.

"He's dangerous, there was no reason for –" Lunar said.

"Now just wait – " Kes said.

"EVERYBODY CALM DOWN!" Sorrel shouted. Rapt said something under his breath and stepped forward, bringing the gun to his shoulder. In one smooth movement Rashelope raised and swung her shovel. She hit him across the face. He fell without a sound, his dark glasses clattering on the cave floor, the gun still in his hand. Rashelope grabbed it, ran her fingers along the side of the weapon, unhooked a small catch and pointed it at the entrance. She pulled the trigger. Nothing happened. "It's not loaded," she said. "No more dangerous than a tree branch." She threw the gun to the ground and resumed her place next to Emrallie.

"Sorrel, tend to Sarane. Make sure the wound is clean. Don't waste the water," Emrallie said. "You," she pointed at Kes, "have one of your band see to him."

Rapt stirred. His right eye had gone red and was beginning to swell. Sorrel went to the pile of backpacks to get her machete. She wondered where Caroni was.

She found a piece of cloth in her pack and went to Sarane outside. She called to Pia to bring one of the torches.

Sarane leant against a rock with her eyes closed and her face turned upwards. The cut near her hairline was small but deep, still bleeding. "Good thing you don't have any hair," Sorrel said. "Helps prevent infection." She didn't know if this was true. "I think we should use a bit of that sap from the tree in Jiba to hold the cut closed," she said.

"Do you have any?"

"Emrallie has a lot – she's been storing it for months. We'll have to soften it in the sun tomorrow. Let's go back inside now."

"Sorrel? I'm *starving*. We need food."

"I know," Sorrel said. "I'll look for the sap."

Inside, the females and males sat randomly – some in small groups, others by themselves. Rapt leaned against the cave wall near the entrance, dark glasses on. She could see the bruise where Rashelope had hit him, spreading onto his swollen cheek and along his jaw.

Journey and Slate sat together in the darkest part of the cave, close to one of the tunnels. Emrallie and Rashelope were with them, as if on guard. *They're getting ready to run, if this doesn't go their way*, thought Sorrel. There was still no sign of Caroni. Her stomach contracted. She thought of the food they had, wrapped in old cloth, hidden behind a rock in the darkest part of the cave, and she wanted all of it for herself.

She rooted around in her backpack, looking for the sap, stored in the discarded shell of some long dead animal. When she found it, she walked outside and put the shell on a rock with the opening facing upwards. Was putting it on a wound a good idea? She was buried in ignorance and uncertainty. She felt Rapt's eyes on her.

And she hated the inaction. She wanted a decision, whatever it was, a plan, a destination, some action. She returned to the cave and went to stand over to Rapt. "How's your eye?"

She wanted to intimidate him. He stared straight ahead and didn't answer but the muscles in his jaw were working and, despite his air of relaxation, he was tense. Explosive. *So am I,* she thought.

She hadn't felt the same threat from Kes, but she could be wrong about him. She knew too little about males. She went to sit with Emrallie and Rashelope. The only sound was the slow drip of water from the cave roof into the bowls.

"Sorrel?" Lichen said, walking over to the three of them. "I think we should all eat something. P-people are drinking, but not eating. Where's the f-food?"

"You're right but let's try to wait through tonight." She

wondered if the males had food with them. She didn't want them to see where the band's food was hidden. Come back Caroni, she whispered to herself.

Caroni and her group of girls returned at dawn, stumbling into the cave. They had set watches and Sorrel's had been the last. The males had done the same thing. "Nothing?" she said to the Zorah, relieving her of her pack.

The Zorah shook her head. She leaned against the cave wall, breathing heavily. "We just ran into a sheer cliff face. Almost as smooth as ice. Maybe part of a fault line. We can't climb over it, not even with ropes."

Sorrel told her about the males. "How many did you say?" Caroni asked. She looked incapable of surprise.

"Four. One had a gun, but it turned out to be unloaded. There was a skirmish, but I think we're all okay. We didn't eat, though. I didn't want them to see the food."

"You did right."

Slowly, everyone woke. Kes came over and spoke directly to Caroni. "You're the leader, right?" he said without preamble. "I'm Kes. We don't mean you any harm, despite what happened. We can just go our separate ways now."

Caroni looked at him. "Do you have food with you?"

"Some," he admitted.

"Shall we share what we have now? Together?"

Kes didn't answer. No one else spoke and the silence lengthened. Rapt cursed under his breath.

"Lichen, go and get our food," Caroni said. "Let's move closer to the entrance. Sorrel, boot up the PlAK." She turned to Kes. "We have something to show you."

They sat in circles around the PlAK and a small pile of food. The males had emptied their pockets and added their rations. "Should we eat first?" Kes asked Caroni.

"After."

Sorrel showed him all that they had seen on the PlAK. The dust storm was closer, now the shape of a pear on its side. Two ships had passed the nearby island of Ayiti. "Northerners are coming to Bajacu," Caroni said, pointing.

142

Kes sat back on his heels. "Here? Why?"

"We're not sure, but it looks like the situation on the continents is worse. We still have mountains and rain. Maybe they've struck a deal with the Domins. Or they'll just moor their ships in our harbour."

"Okay, fine, but I'm less worried about them – who says they're going to get up here anyway – but that dust storm looks bad. We're going to get stuck in this cave with almost no food."

"We need to join forces," Caroni said. "Don't you see? We need to take the Toplander camp. It's defensible, there's water, they're growing food, and if the satellites come down, it's a high vantage point. We could settle there."

Kes shook his head. "You don't know what you're saying. What it would take."

"Let's at least talk about it," Caroni said. "What kind of food do you have?" She reached over and opened the Tribals's wrapped food. "Alganola. Even dried fruit."

Sorrel's stomach cramped. She wanted to grab all the food and run.

CHAPTER 27 – TUNNEL

After everyone had eaten their rations – the males had something they called "jerky", which was as tasteless as cardboard, but somehow made them feel stronger – they sat around Caroni and Kes.

"Rashelope, tell us what you saw at Cibao," said the Zorah.

"It's fortified. Defended. A stone wall right around, men with guns behind it. The PlAK would show more than I saw from the ground. It's reachable. Maybe four hours travel from here for most of us. We did see one place where the wall was a bit broken down near to a gully, probably from storm water. A decent entry point. But I don't know how many Toplanders there are, how well armed, nothing like that. We can get there from here, that's all I can really say."

"It's closer from our camp," Kes said. "Two-three hours."

"If we go to their camp, they'll outnumber us," Rashelope said to Caroni, pointing at the males. "Take our stuff. Maybe kill us, just like that one over there was willing to do."

"We're not going to kill you," Kes said. "We want – "

"They'll want the PlAK and Sorrel," Caroni cut in. "They don't have anyone who can get into Level 2, much less Level 1. And that's what'll give us the information we need if we're going to think about taking the army camp."

"So you – we – are going to just trust them? *Males*?" Rashelope said. "What do they have that we want?"

"Numbers. Guns. Ammunition. Knowledge of the terrain. Physical strength," Caroni said.

"We can't live with *males*," Emrallie said.

"We're just people," Journey said. "Most of us had sisters."

"I don't see that we have a choice," Sorrel said. "We can't stay here. There's no food in their valley. Maybe together we can take Cibao. Especially if we have satellite information to guide us."

"Quick death versus slow death." Rashelope said.

"Maybe," Caroni said. She looked at her hands. "I need an hour to think. It's too hot to travel right now anyway." She walked towards the back of the cave. "Leave me."

"Okay," Kes said. "One hour. Then we're leaving with or without you."

Sorrel put the PlAK on charge and sat, looking out. It was hazy again and she thought about the coming dust. "Should we take down the ropes?" Emrallie said, joining her.

"When we know what's happening."

"Males. I don't know."

Sorrel didn't answer. They sat together as the minutes ticked by.

When Caroni came back, they all turned to her. She stood straight and her head was held high. "Let's get ready to leave with them. I need to speak with their leader," she said. "Fill the algaskins from the water in the bowls. Drink the rest." She faced Rashelope, who met her gaze with a steady, unflinching stare.

Then Rashelope lowered her eyes and stepped back. "Zorah," she said. It struck Sorrel how rarely they used Caroni's title.

"Shall I take down the ropes now?" Emrallie said.

"Yes. Let's not make it easy for anyone else to find us."

"Shouldn't we wait?" Lichen said. "It's really h-hot outside."

"We'll lead you through the tunnel," Kes said. "By the time we get to the sinkhole, it'll be dusk."

The women formed a line, a hand on each other's shoulders. The males held the torches, running their fingers along the walls, feeling for the marks they had made. They had walked for less than ten minutes when Kes stopped and said, "Here's the entrance to our tunnel." It was a narrow, slanted space amidst a rockfall, deep in the shadows cast by the torchlight. No wonder Emrallie's group hadn't found it.

They took off their backpacks and torches and passed them through the space. The new tunnel was low and close and airless.

It seemed to wind and double back on itself. Sorrel gave herself up to the journey, touching Emrallie in front of her, feeling Sarane's hand from behind on her own shoulder. *Quick death, slow death,* she thought.

After uncounted hours, there was a subtle lightening in the darkness and the males in front stopped, looking upwards. Sorrel saw the grey of the night sky above them and felt fresh air on her face. She breathed deeply. The torchlight glinted on the metal of the old ladder Kes had described. He whistled and there was an answering whistle. "Geo? Mando?" he called out.

"*Guata* man. We thought you were lost."

"Where's the rope?"

"We pulled it up."

"Suppose we were being chased?"

There was no answer but a thick rope with knots tied at regular intervals fell into the cave. "Journey, you go up first. Tell them we have strangers with us. Females," Kes said.

"*Females?*" said the voice above.

Journey climbed the rope easily, hand over hand. Would all the females be able to follow? Many were so weak now. Sorrel filled her lungs and watched how the males climbed the rope, snaking up it like one of the caterpillar-type insects they used to eat. According to Kes, they were going to a place where all the birds and insects had been killed and eaten. She remembered her first sight of the ravine where she had lived for almost a year and felt a lancing, immobilizing loss. Then it was her turn to climb. "I'll give you a little boost," Kes said, at her side. His breath was warm on her cheek.

"It's not necessary," she said, turning away. "Help the two you injured. And Pia."

There was a pale full moon that night and the male camp had an abandoned look. Half of it was in the deep shadow of the cliffs that created the valley, eerie in the faint moonlight. There were no sounds at all. *They killed all the insects,* Sorrel thought.

"Wait here," Kes said to the Tribals. "Sorrel and Caroni, you come with me." The three other males stepped forward to join Kes, but Rashelope barred their way. "You wait with us," she said. Kes nodded at them.

He led the way to one of the lean-tos they'd seen on the PlAK. "They're decoys," he explained. *Of course*, Sorrel thought. No one would have been able to shelter in the day under a lean-to, no matter how high in the mountains they were, nor would they be any use in a rain bomb or hurricane.

Kes ducked into one of the shelters, made with long sticks fastened to a frame. "These are things we can afford to lose," he said, kicking at a pile of tool handles.

"We made those into weapons," Sorrel said. *You're wasteful*, she wanted to add.

'I saw that," he said.

"Where d'you all live then?"

"You'll see."

Kes whistled and the sound was shocking in the silent valley. A male walked out of the shadows, carrying a gun. "Where is everybody?" he said, looking around. Then: "*Guata*. Females? Did something happen?"

"We found a female band in the cave under the sinkhole…"

"You did not *find* us. We were there already," Caroni snapped.

"Fine," Kes said. "We met. Encountered. Whatever. This is Sandstorm." He gestured. "Caroni and Sorrel."

"How many of them are there?"

"Sixteen. Go get Arc. Can I bring everyone in now?"

"Better not," said Sandstorm. "Wait until Arc is here."

Sorrel felt like sitting in the grass but didn't want to appear weak. Sandstorm returned with another man, also carrying a gun. "What's all this?" he said. "What have you got us into, Kes? You had simple orders –"

"The first thing you could all do is put down the *guatan* guns," Caroni said. The Zorah rarely swore.

"They were in the cave," Kes said. "The one the sinkhole leads to. They had to leave the ravine; they said there was no food there anymore. They have a PlAK and this woman here –" he pointed to Sorrel, "can hack into real time. Level 1. They're starving too. There's a dust storm coming. And an invasion. I brought them back with us because maybe we'd be better together. Kes gestured at the second man, who looked bewildered. "This is Arc, our leader."

147

The male leader was nearly two metres tall but stood hunched over as if trying to hide his height. He wore a thin T-shirt and Sorrel could see his ribs.

"Greetings," he said to the two females. "That's a lot to take in. An invasion, you said?"

"Well, take it in," Caroni said. "We're here. We can go and talk alone about the invasion and everything else, or we can go to wherever you all shelter and get some rest until the morning. Please decide."

Arc lowered his eyes and his face was in shadow. "Alright," he said. "Sandstorm will take you to a cave where you can spend the night. Rest for a few hours. The camp rises at 0400 hours. You mount a guard and we'll do the same, until we've had a chance to talk."

"Go and get everyone, Sorrel," Caroni said.

Sandstorm led the females to a cliff face. "There's the entrance," he said, pointing. "It's narrow."

"Sorrel, take the PlAK. Leave your backpack with me. Go inside and have a look around," Caroni said from in front.

Sorrel shrugged her pack off and was glad to be free of its weight. She was tired to her bones. She eased herself through the fissure and turned on the PlAK. The searchlight was dim but adequate and revealed a smallish, empty cave with a sandy floor. She couldn't imagine how sand came to be this high in the mountains.

"Looks fine," she called to Caroni.

"It's our sentry cave," Sandstorm said.

One by one, the Tribals passed their loads into the cave and then slid in themselves.

"We have to be ready for tomorrow," Caroni said. "Who'll take the first watch?"

"I will," Rashelope said.

Sorrel stood alone with her back to the entrance, waiting for her night vision to settle.

"I found a good spot," Emrallie said beside her. "Come. Time to sleep."

She followed her friend to the back of the cave, where there was a thicker pile of sand, like a small dune. Sorrel laid her backpack beside her and stretched out on her ground sheet, now thin from wear, her hand on the handle of her machete, glad for Rashelope's presence at the mouth of the cave.

RESISTANCE

2085

CHAPTER 28 – COUNCIL

The males called it their council meeting. The two leaders had talked alone before bringing everyone together in a much larger cave, also with a sandy floor. They sat in concentric circles around Caroni and Arc. Torches flickered on the walls. Arc had tired eyes, brown hair tied in a ponytail with a shoelace and a full beard. Facial hair was unusual, and Sorrel wondered if he had grown up elsewhere – somewhere away from the plastic soup the sea had become. He seemed the oldest of the males, with a few flecks of gray in his hair and beard, and she wondered about their rules regarding old people. There was a flat rock in the middle of the circle. Arc sat with Caroni in the sand, leaning against the rock.

Sorrel wished she'd been allowed to sleep for longer. Her muscles burned and her eyes felt gritty. She thought of her mother for the thousandth time. Was she still alive? What trials might she be facing in this hour before dawn, wherever she was?

Across the circle, she met Kes's eyes. He smiled and mouthed something. His gaze made her uncomfortable and she looked away. Rapt sat in the outermost circle, wearing his dark glasses. *Males in the flesh*, she thought. It felt like a dream.

"I've heard your story from your leader," Arc nodded at Caroni, looking around as he spoke, "and now we welcome you here. I know two of your band have been hurt, as has one of ours. We hope that's an end to violence between us."

He paused. "We were members of a Lowlander chat group and we came together from all over Bajacu to see if we could live at higher altitudes. Some of us," Arc indicated the youngest-looking boy, "are family. A few of us had been selected for the Squad and we didn't want to go. We've been in the hills for six years and survived feral attacks, Domin ranger patrols, rain bombs, land-

153

slides, dust storms. We used to be bigger – we lost seven people last year in a landslide." He paused.

"We're sixteen now," Caroni said. "We've had our trials too."

"We have water in this valley, but it's declining. When it's light, we'll show you the waterfall. And you can see we have good shelter in these caves. We built the lean-tos you saw as decoys –"

"You shouldn't have built them," Rashelope interrupted. "That's how we found you."

"This is the one who injured Rapt?" Arc said, turning to Caroni.

"He was threatening –"

"She'll be useful. You saw us," he continued, "but you couldn't get to us from the south, right? Except for the tunnel from the sinkhole to the cave, there's only one way into this valley overland and few have found it so far. The lean-tos distract anyone who comes. They dig through the stuff, take what they want and leave. We post sentries day and night. We have guns and other weapons."

"Do you have ammunition?" Caroni asked.

"Some. Maybe enough, maybe not."

Enough for what, Sorrel wondered.

"For a while we had enough to eat and there was the camp above. We started to raid it. There were not many Toplanders there at first. But then they built the wall and more started to come."

"I told them about Alba and Llando," Kes said.

"Tell us more about the camp," Caroni said.

"Well, you know it's an old army camp, right? We found a busted-up sign in an old drain – it was called Cibao in the Renaming. It's on a very steep part of the mountain – hard to understand why they built it there, really. We haven't tried a raid in at least a year, but what we saw in the early days was a few ruined buildings, some foundations, and some newer houses – built well, with roofs and solar panels. A really old cemetery. A spring. A big cement area, cracked up, which might have been a parade ground. They use its surfaces to channel rainwater into cisterns. They grow things and raise animals in wire cages. We saw skynut trees; a whole section of succulents, presumably for soap or salve for sunburn. Then there's the wall. The roads were destroyed in a landslide before we came here. Cibao is easy to defend."

"What about the people? You said they were old?"

"In the beginning. Now the walls have young males on them, looking out, patrolling. Some have binoculars."

"They're on the wall even in the day?" Caroni said.

"Yes. You'll be amazed at what 500 metres of altitude does to the temperature. They can't stay outside all day, of course, so they have shifts."

"What kind of young males? asked Rashelope.

"What kind? I don't know. Young men. Well fed. Strong. Last time we tried a raid, they killed two of ours. Cut off the head of one and laughed."

"I mean, are they trained?" Rashelope said. "Ex Domins? Ex Squad?"

"I don't know about their training. They definitely have more weapons than we do, but we don't know about their ammunition."

"Are there females?" Rashelope said.

"We've seen some working outside, mostly with the food they grow."

"Slaves?" Sorrel asked. Everyone turned to look at her.

Arc shrugged. "We've heard the stories too. What we saw – and remember, this isn't recent – was females working with the crops and males nearby with guns or other weapons." He turned his head to look at Sorrel. "Why?"

"It's not important right now," Caroni said, glaring at Sorrel.

"That's our story; more or less," Arc concluded. "We've been sending out smaller groups to see if we can find a new place to settle because there's less and less food here."

"Like us. We can find out a lot more about the camp with a PlAK and someone with Level 1 access," Caroni said.

"Why're you so interested in the camp? It's a fortress. Believe me, we've tried to get in there. It can't be done."

"I hear you."

"Time for your story now," Arc said.

Sorrel half listened to Caroni's voice, telling of Jiba, their time there and the new threats. "Sorrel can hack into Level 1. That's how we found out the Northerners are coming. And saw the dust storm."

"Show me," Arc said, staring at her.

She met his eyes. "We have to act quickly," she said. "The Northerners are disabling the satellites."

CHAPTER 29 – THE WATERFALL

Sorrel's back hurt from poring over the PlAK with Arc for more than two hours. They had started as soon as it was light enough and it had been slow work, because the signal was intermittent, and the screen kept pixelating or freezing. She saw dawn jump across the world in fits and starts. The ships had all detached from the land and become part of the ocean. They had gone in different directions – some heading north, hugging the new coastline of Amerika, some travelling east across the Ocean of Atlantis, some towards the Sea of the Antilles. The first ship heading in their direction was well past Ayiti now. The edge of the dust storm was just touching Boriken. "No more than two days away," she said.

The screen froze again. Her hair was growing, and her scalp itched. "I need to stand up," she said to Arc. "And the PlAK needs charging."

Caroni sat nearby, watching them. Everyone else was asleep in small mounds.

"Get some sleep, Sorrel," Caroni said.

"It's hard for me to sleep in the day. I need to walk for a little. I'm really stiff."

The Zorah nodded.

Sorrel left the cave. The sense of danger and unease which had started in the rain as they left Jiba was growing. Would it be easier to die of hunger? How long would that take? She remembered facing the rain bomb at the cable car and knowing she'd prefer to die fighting.

The grass was wet and shiny; *dew*, she remembered. She thought it a beautiful word, like waterfall. The sky had a yellowish cast. Her stomach griped; she couldn't remember when last she had eaten a proper meal. How many centuries would pass before humans would be able to survive on grass?

She heard soft footfalls behind her and swung around, expecting Rapt, and fear rose to her throat, but it was Kes, wiping sleep from his eyes. "D'you want to see the waterfall?" he asked. She nodded, flushed with relief. He led her past the tents to a track at the edge of the valley.

"The path is rough," he said, holding out his hand. She took it. His palm was dry and rough. She felt suddenly short of breath.

There was not enough room for them to walk abreast and soon he dropped her hand. The rocky trail wound between the trunks of dead trees and clumps of undergrowth and vines, looking much like Jiba after the river started to fall. The plants were wet and so was the air and she liked the feeling of moisture on her skin. Her hand still felt warm from Kes's palm.

The trail forked and Kes followed the left-hand path. "Where does the other way lead?" Sorrel asked.

"Up the hill to your right. We have a good view of the south wall of the camp from there."

They came to a circular clearing and there, ahead of her, was the misty waterfall she had seen in the PlAK's screen, falling white from the top of a high cliff onto tiers of glistening grey rock and then into a deep green pool.

They stood together. "It used to be bigger," Kes said. She wanted him to stand closer.

"Do you want to swim?" he asked. "We could, but we have to do it right now, before the others wake up. We use this water for drinking."

"I don't want to swim," she said. "Thank you for bringing me here. It's peaceful. Hopeful."

"Shall I leave you alone?"

"No. Stay. We can go back together."

After some time, she left Kes's side and walked to the edge of the pool, loving the heavier spray on her skin, listening to the ceaseless sound of falling water. Her body felt like a bell, struck again and again. Then she heard something impossible in this place and time – music. She turned. Kes sat on a rock with a small musical instrument at his mouth. She couldn't remember its name. He held it in his cupped hands and blew into it, his head tilted to one side. The music was plaintive and sweet and somehow melded with the sound of the waterfall. She wanted to sit close to him, to feel the warmth of his body against hers, to push away all that was facing them. *Fool*, she thought, angry with herself. This kind of *guatan* foolishness will get you killed.

"Let's go back before it gets too hot," she said.

They separated before they got to the big cave. Everyone was up and food was being shared. A liquid was being spooned into smaller bowls and handed out. "What's that?" she asked Emrallie, who was sitting beside her.

"Slate trapped a bird. They made a broth."

There was more of the jerky, which Slate explained was made from dried meat – mostly rodent. "It lasts long if you smoke it," he said. "How did you dry this fruit?"

"Laid them on some flat rocks in the s-sun," Lichen said.

"Didn't avians steal them?"

"We had to post guards."

"Have you ever managed to kill and eat a feral?" Rashelope said.

"Once," Slate said. "A canine. It was an injured baby; puppy, I think they're called. Bigger than a rodent, though. We've tried to hunt them but…"

"But what?" Rashelope said.

"Never been able to track them. Whenever we've caught something that could be feral, we've eaten it."

"Did they show you where the latrines were?" Sorrel asked Emrallie.

"Yes. Didn't you see them when you went out with Kes?"

Sorrel lowered her head, her cheeks warm. "Show me?"

When they got back, Rapt stood at the front of the cave and the light fell on his face. It was black and purple, like a rotten fruit.

Arc and Caroni leaned against the flat rock together and their faces were grave. "You all know the situation. We'll die from starvation if we don't do something," Arc said. "We have to try to take the camp. Maybe we have the numbers to do it now."

"But there's no time to lose," Caroni added. "There's a dust cloud approaching – two days away at most. After it gets here, we may not be able to travel for a while. We told you about the satellites being disabled – soon we'll lose that opportunity as well."

"We have to attack the Toplanders at Cibao, and defeat them this time," Arc said.

Attack, Sorrel thought, and the word nested inside her fear. She had never attacked another person. She would defend herself, certainly, but… She shivered and saw Rapt turn to stare at her.

"Kes and the recce group will go out this afternoon," Arc said. "They'll make sure we can get to where Cibao's wall is crumbling easily. Sometimes the gully gets washed out in the rain and has to be cleared. We don't want to have to dig our way to Cibao."

"Fine. But we can't just pour over a guarded wall together," Caroni said. "We need some kind of diversion."

"Agreed. What do you suggest?"

"Sorrel should use the rest of today to find out exactly what we're facing – how many buildings, people, any weak areas, where the weapons and ammunition might be held," Caroni said. "This meeting is premature. Let the recce group go out and come back and report. Sorrel should do her work and we meet again at dusk."

Arc looked tense. "I'll have my men count our guns and weapons. Ammunition too."

"I'll help," Rashelope said. "You have more things that could be made into weapons in the lean-tos."

"We don't have time for that," Caroni said.

"I could make a start," Pia said. "I'm good with tools. I can make a blade from an old shovel in an hour, less if I have a good hammer."

"I'll go with the recce," Emrallie said.

"I can start putting together supplies," Journey said.

"My mother is in that camp," Sorrel said, and everyone turned to look at her. "She was taken by the Toplanders. I don't want her to be killed. Nor the others they enslaved."

"Now is not the time –" Caroni began.

"How old is your *mother*?" Rapt sneered. "What good is she to anyone?"

Sorrel jumped to her feet and faced him. "She *raised* me. Didn't you have a mother?"

"Sorrel, enough," Caroni snapped. "We've spoken about your mother before. Sometimes –" She stopped. "Go and use the PlAK. Help us to make this work. It's the only chance for *everybody* here."

Rapt strode into the back of the cave. He hadn't been given a task. *He's easy with killing,* Sorrel thought. He *wants* to kill. He's like the males who laughed over the old woman's body in Bana. She was sure he'd had violence training. She looked around at the other faces; most were solemn and fearful, some expressionless, others hidden.

"We don't have a choice, people," Caroni said. "We have to find a way to do this. We're able to survey the camp with the PlAK. We have surprise on our side; young males and females, weapons – "

"You don't want to fight, though. That's what this talk is all about," Rapt said.

Arc stood up. "*Guata,* man. Be quiet. It's nearly peak heat. Is the PlAK on charge?"

"Yes. It'll need an hour," Sorrel said.

"Kes, get your group together and go," Arc said. "Be back by dusk. Clear any obstacles in the gully as you go and then time how fast you can get back. Walking speed though. Don't run."

"The rest of you, get Sorrel some stones," Caroni said. "Different sizes. Twigs. She's going to need something to count and draw a basic map in the sand. We go tomorrow night."

No one moved. She clapped her hands impatiently. "Let's go!"

CHAPTER 30 – TOPLANDERS

Sorrel lay against her pack, waiting for the PlAK to charge, thinking of Toplanders. She was so hungry. Bird broth, jerky, dried insects, a few pieces of dried fruit were just not enough.

The tech centre in Bana had been owned by a Toplander. She had seen him once – a well-fed male with floppy hair which seemed to say, *The rest of you are bald; I don't have to be*. He wore new clothes and his eyes had moved over her without stopping. She meant nothing to him. Maybe elites were the same everywhere; they took what they wanted, be it territory, food or sex. She wished she'd paid more attention to modules about war.

The recce group had left, Emrallie with them. She remembered the shining waterfall and heard Kes's music, sweet and true and dying away. Her eyelids drooped.

Lichen woke her. "The P-PlAK is charged, Sorrel. Time to get up. I brought you some water."

"Thanks. What time is it?"

"Mid-afternoon."

"Did they get the stones?"

"Yes. They're over there."

She settled down next to piles of stones and leaves and sticks and began her work. Two more satellites gone. She could no longer see the edges of the dust cloud – it was now a vast orange haze over Bajacu, Boriken and Ayiti, spreading north as far as the tip of Coabana. They had even less time than she'd thought.

She drew the shape of the encircling wall in the sand. Then she zoomed in closer to the camp, putting a stone aside for each figure as she spotted them. She assumed the smallest were females, but sometimes it was hard to be sure. One figure appeared to be digging close to one of the buildings, while another watched. She counted all the larger figures as males. Some of the guards stood looking out; others sat on the wall, their legs dangling over. All the guards carried something in their hands – guns, she guessed, or other types of weapon. She made a pile of twigs for weapons. The guards were not evenly spaced on the wall and she wondered why.

She drew the evenly laid out patches of crops in the sand. Several plastic water tanks were scattered throughout the camp and she marked them with stones. Small figures moved around the garden patches and she counted all of those as females. She strained to see if any one of them could be Bibi, but they were too tiny. The images on the PlAK froze and she sat back on her heels and waited.

She followed the walls that surrounded the camp and saw the lower section that Arc had talked about – only two guards on that side – and a faint trace of the gully they would use to approach. She began to add shapes for the buildings to her map. Some were rectangular – probably where people slept. There were ordinary looking old-time houses, a few much bigger than others. Something that looked like a church. One blocky building with a flat roof, close to the part of the wall where most of the guards were clustered. *I bet that's where they keep the weapons and ammunition*, she thought. She wished she could see better. There was another flat-roofed building, square and low, half sunk in the ground. She drew the paths she could see on the map.

The image froze and failed resolve. The battery was almost dead – it would soon fail completely. She plugged the PlAK into the charger and stared at the map she'd made in the sand. It was an insubstantial thing to use for life and death decisions. They needed something more.

She went to find Rapt.

He sat alone under one the lean-tos and for the first time, she felt a twinge of sympathy for him. He was a teenager, like her, and perhaps if he had been a Squaddie, had never heard a caring word. "I want to ask you something," she said and sat beside him.

"*You* want to ask *me* something?"

"Yes. About war. About fighting. Were you violence-trained?"

"What d'you think?" She thought she saw tears in his undamaged eye.

"That must really hurt," she said, pointing to his injury.

He shrugged. "Yes, I was in the camps. I was five when they took me."

"You had to study battle techniques, right?"

"So what?"

"I'm pretty sure there are enslaved women in Cibao. Suppose we could get them on our side? We'd have people to fight on the inside as well. More numbers. Wouldn't that improve our chances?"

Rapt didn't answer right away. He seemed lost in thought. Then he said in the softest tone she had heard him use: "Yes, it probably would. Especially if they were armed. But even if not armed, they would know the layout of the camp better than us."

She nodded. "I think there are about thirty women in the camp."

"Not all would join us," he said. "And there's no time to negotiate with them, anyway. When we attack, there's going to be nothing but confusion." He shrugged. "Good thinking all the same."

"I have some aloe in my pack. It's soothing. Would you like some for your cheek? Don't get it in your eyes, though."

"I don't need it." He turned away, but she thought he whispered "thanks" as she left.

CHAPTER 31 – DUST STORM

She sat in the council meeting after the recce group returned. They described the route they'd taken, and she memorized the landmarks as they spoke – a dead tree with branches like claws, a landslide, a pile of rusting car doors, a water tank with a jagged hole in the side. She'd seen only some of them on the PlAK. "One hour's journey," Kes said. "On the way back. Might take a little longer at night."

Then it was her turn. She took Arc and Caroni over to the map she'd made and described the basic layout of the camp, where most guards were clustered. She'd counted nine guards, another nineteen males, maybe thirty women. "There might have been some people inside the buildings as well, so I wouldn't have counted those," she finished.

"Smaller numbers than I thought," Arc said.

"And the dust storm?" Caroni said. "I can smell it now."

"It's spread out over a wider area. Seems not to be as thick, but thick enough in the middle. I figure it will reach us tomorrow night."

"Should we go tonight, then?" Arc said.

"We can't," Emrallie said. "We're too tired. If we're to have a chance we need to eat and sleep. The earliest we can go is dusk tomorrow."

"Maybe the dust will help us," Rashelope said.

"We don't know what equipment the Toplanders have. They could have PlAKs too," Sorrel said. She felt Rapt's eyes on her and she knew he was wondering why she didn't speak about trying to get the captured women on their side. She shook her head and he said nothing.

"The dust will keep most people inside," Caroni said. "Except for the guards."

"Maybe that's a good reason for not having a diversion," Arc said. "Noise will bring people out."

"What's the alternative, though? One to one combat? Trying to kill each guard with a knife, with as little noise as possible? Do we have the right people to do that?" Caroni said.

"We need to find their leaders," Rapt said. "Kill or capture them and we have a chance."

"How will we do that in the dark in the middle of a dust storm?" Arc said.

"Torture somebody," Rapt said.

Sorrel looked around. Few were paying attention to what was being said. The atmosphere in the cave felt resigned, even hopeless. Rashelope and Emrallie had fallen silent.

The odds were long whatever they did. As the discussion went on, the idea of a diversion was rejected. They would pour over the wall from the gully, kill the nearby guards, and spread out in fan formation, trying to find Colonel Drax and other leaders. Torture was not mentioned again. Talk wound down, and slowly the males and females drifted away from the council circle.

After everyone was asleep, Sorrel took her machete and knife, her algaskin and a few pieces of dried fruit she had saved from her ration but left her backpack behind. Let everyone think she had wandered off for a few minutes. As she passed the lean-tos she saw a torn camouflage shirt and she put it on. Maybe it would fool the Toplanders for a moment.

The moon was a faint glimmer in the grey sky, veiled by the dust haze. Broken branches marked the way the recce group had taken, and she fell into her stride. She needed to get to the camp's wall in less than three hours. She started to taste the dust in the back of her throat.

She had never been so alone in the bush and the silence was unnerving. She startled at her own sounds, listening for ferals. To distract herself, she went through what she might find in the camp: would she have to kill one of the guards to get in? What was the best way to do that? What if she got caught? What would they do to her if she was captured? What would Caroni and the others think when they found she was not there? Was Bibi still alive? And if she wasn't, why would any of the Lowlander females listen to her?

She almost bumped into the dead tree ahead. This was where she had to climb. She untied her scarf, wet it with water from the algaskin and tied it over her nose and mouth. She used her gloved hands on the steeper slope to scramble upwards.

She climbed until she came across the gully that Kes and the others had described and slid down a steep, sandy slope. Her thighs and calves were burning, and her head swam with the exertion.

She found the stone wall around Cibao just as she was at the limit of her strength. The dust was beginning to settle on the land, and she could taste grit in her mouth. She came upon a jagged rock off to one side, and rested behind it, waiting for her breath to quieten. She remembered her fight with the porc. *Stop thinking*, she told herself.

She circled the base of the wall as quietly as she could, glad for the muffling effect of the dust, looking for where the nearest guards were. She thought she saw one in the distance but couldn't decide whether his back was turned or not. *Just do it*, she whispered to herself. *Behave like you belong here.* She pulled the camouflage shirt close and straightened up. She decided to make for the rectangular building nearest to patches of plantings. That, she hoped, would be where the women slept. She kept the satellite images in her mind and clambered over the crumbling wall.

The other side was deep in the shadow and she hunkered down for a moment. There, to her right, was the half-buried building. Farther away, she could just make out the square structure she'd thought might hold their weapons and ammunition with the path beside it. She marched through the middle of the camp in what she hoped was the direction of the rectangular buildings.

She approached one building, but it was too small. The windows and doors were all closed. She traced her hand along the wall and walked around it, gravel crunching underfoot, the sound mostly muffled by the dust. Another building loomed up; was this the right one? The dust was disorienting her.

She explored the exterior with her fingers. The walls were made of planks of wood and there were windows at regular intervals with closed shutters. The doors at each end of the building were shut. There was a low wall at one end of it, half hidden by a prickly bush. She sat on the wall in the deeper shadow of the building, trying to decide what to do. Then she smelled ripe fruit. Her stomach clenched, and saliva flooded her mouth. She peered at the branches, wishing she had a source of light, and saw clumps of tiny berries. She pulled them off the bush in handfuls, stuffing them into her mouth. She felt the pain of their sweetness in her temples and remembered her first taste of coconut water.

A nearby door banged open and she shrank into the bush. She could just see the shape of a woman stepping out onto the grass, rubbing her face. The figure stumbled to a small building at the limit of Sorrel's vision and went inside.

She stood and waited for the woman to return.

She heard her returning footsteps before she saw her. She was almost at the door. Sorrel whispered, "Wait!"

"Who's there? Is that you, LT? I was just –" The woman sounded terrified.

"No, it's me." Sorrel approached the woman, palms outward.

"What? Who are you?" She stumbled on the low step into the building as she tried to retreat.

Sorrel went right up to her. "I won't hurt you. I'm a Lowlander, looking for my mother."

"Are you crazy?" the female hissed. "They'll kill you! How did you get into the camp?"

"It's a long story. Who's inside? Are you all females? Lowlanders?"

"Yes. You'd better come inside. LT will be along on patrol in seconds, although he won't be liking this dust."

The door creaked open and they slipped inside. It was as dark as the back of a cave. The woman lit a candle. Old-time metal beds were lined up against the walls, the ones closest to where they stood were empty. Sorrel could hear the steady breathing of people, probably asleep. "I have to find a place to hide you," the woman whispered. "Come with me. I'm going to wake up Iris and Petal and you can tell us your story."

Flower names, Sorrel thought. These females are from Bana.

The woman led her to a corner at one end of the building. "Sit," she whispered, and stood with one ear against the wood. Sorrel could hear nothing from outside. She slid to the floor, leaning against the wall and listened to the women breathe.

After a short time, the woman squatted beside her. "I think he's gone. He won't be back for half an hour, maybe more. You stay here."

"What's your name?"

"Selan."

"I'm Sorrel. From Bana."

"Huh. I'll be right back," Selan said.

She returned with two other females. "Sit in a close circle," she said. "Knees touching." Sorrel complied, and the women leaned in together. Selan whispered. "So who are you and what're you doing here?"

Sorrel gathered her thoughts. "I came to the mountains with my mother from Bana because we heard it was cooler. We found a group of Tribals, a female band. I stayed with them; my mother left. I'm here to find her."

"Why would your mother be here?" Selan said. "Why should we trust you?" She had a wide scar on her cheek from ear to mouth.

"We should sound the alarm," said one of the other females. She had a baby face with round cheeks. "If we're found with a fugitive, you know what's going to happen to us."

"I know my mother was here. She sent me a message."

"I'm Petal. From Bana too," the third woman said. "Easy to check her story, Selan. You – what's your mother's name?"

Sorrel didn't answer right away.

"Well?" Selan demanded. "Or is your whole story a lie?"

"Bibi," Sorrel said. "Bibi Morgan."

There was silence. "She was captured a year ago," Selan said.

"Is she here then?" Sorrel said.

"She's in detainment."

"Detainment?

"Prison. Punishment. Torture, probably. Colonel Drax takes a woman, one of us, every few weeks. We never know when it's coming, and we never know who's next. He thinks it keeps the rest of us in line. It was your mother's turn yesterday."

CHAPTER 32 – BIBI

They found me at dawn. I almost drowned but managed to keep hold of the tree branch that took me downriver. I crawled out on a stony beach where the river curved and there was no more shade from trees or the ravine walls. I was cut up, bleeding. I just lay there, feeling the pebbles starting to warm. I heard barking and I realised canines were close by. There was a whole pack of them around that place; they fed on whatever the river brought down. Then I heard voices and I had no choice, I got up and went towards them. Three Toplanders, all males. Turned out they were just like ferals; came to this place to scavenge dead animals, and stones for their buildings. They tied my hands behind my back and marched me to their camp, following a narrow, twisty dry stream course which still had a few trees.

One said I was too old. Another that a slave woman had died and a replacement was needed. A third told them the colonel would hurt them if they failed to bring a Lowlander to camp and it was for him to decide what happened to me.

I was too grief-stricken to be afraid.

They threw me into a concrete building that was half underground. The sun was well up by then and I thought I would die there. But it was cool in that room. Enough light came under the door to see some details – a bed, a desk and two chairs. An unlit old-time lamp. A bucket in a corner. A shackle hanging down on the wall.

After Colonel Drax came into that room, I learned that everything ends but what comes after an ending can be worse. Pain racks the body, but it's humiliation that brings you true defeat.

They let me stay in the old camp at Cibao and I became their slave. They fed us just enough, because they wanted us to work, and kept us in line just by the memory of our time in the half-buried room where they let us know that anything – anything at all – could be done to us and no one would know or care.

I was glad to be with other women, though. We took it in turn to talk about our children. It was possible to work in the day for most of the year up there in the mountains, so we often slept at night. The last thing we said before going to sleep were the names of our children, whom we knew we'd never see again.

CHAPTER 33 – LOWLANDER WOMEN

The guard the women called LT returned at sunrise. They had hidden Sorrel under a pile of bedding, and she could just hear him say, "No one leaves the barracks today because of the dust. Give me all your algaskins, I'll fill them up. You'll get some soup at midday. Maybe. If I find anyone outside, they'll die and not quickly."

She heard the scraping sound of bolts being pulled across.

"Suppose there's a fire, LT?" one of the women called.

"Then you'll burn up. Settle down now. The dust might not last for long."

Time passed. Sorrel felt sick thinking of Bibi being tortured.

"You can come out now," Selan said eventually. "Here. Drink something. We have extra."

Sorrel took the algaskin and tipped it to her mouth. The water had the same sharp taste as the river in Jiba. The Toplanders seemed to have the best of all things – a clean, running river. She wondered if its level was falling too.

It was getting lighter. The women sat or lay on their beds. They did not seem malnourished, but most had scars on their faces. One was missing an ear, another an eye. Some talked quietly together, others dozed. Some stared at the roof, their hands behind their heads. Petal was weaving thick grass into a round sling. "Macrame," she explained. "Old-time craft. My grandmother showed me how to do it."

"What are you making?"

"A sling for a calabash. The material is *khus-khus* grass, which has many uses. We have dozens of slings; I'm really doing it to pass the time."

"That guard locked us in?"

"Yes. They're afraid we'll run in the dust."

"Will you tell me about the camp? About what's happening to my mother?"

Petal sighed, her fingers flying back and forth. "You really want to know about your mother?"

"Yes," Sorrel said. She watched Petal's hands. Her own were shaking. She sat on them.

"Drax is the colonel here. That's what he calls himself anyway; they like to think of themselves as an army. The original settlers here were all one family, the Nelsons, just what you heard in Bana: rich people who used to be in business; government, before the Domins took over. I think some of them had family houses in the mountains from before the Convergence, so they knew what it was like up here. The Nelson family used to own the tech centres. Maybe still do.

"They needed labour, so they started to capture anyone they could. At first, they caught males, but males were too inclined to fight back so they decided on female slaves, who could also service the men and keep them happy. Colonel Drax is obsessed with military campaigns, especially genocide. He'll read about them to you while he's – " She stopped.

"While he's what?"

"Whatever he's doing. Beating you. Biting. Hanging you from a rafter. Cutting you. You see that scar Selan has? He came to talk to us about what he called a telephone cut – how a cut from ear to mouth that goes right through your cheek takes a long time to heal. How food and water leaks from it. How easily it gets infected. Then he said one of us would get a telephone cut before the week was out. Selan was the one he chose and everything he said about it was true. She almost died.

"And he rapes us, of course. They all do. For the others, it's quick. With the Colonel, the more you scream, the more he likes it. He finds out what you hate most and that's what he'll do to you, over and over and over. Afterwards, he'll ask – do you love me? He'll rest your head on his shoulder and stroke your hair, and he'll read to you about atrocities in history in a loving voice." Petal shuddered.

"That's what's happening to my mother now?"

"Some version of it. I'm sorry. She'll survive, though. It's not her first time. All of us have been through it. We try to stop him taking the youngest girls, but we haven't had a really young girl up here in a long time. Luckily, most of us aren't fertile. Do you want me to go on?"

"No. How many of them are there now?"

"Toplanders? Forty or so. We never see them all at the same time, but that's what we think. A handful are old, I mean, really old. In their sixties. Another twenty are middle aged. They need young males for the walls, and they've lost two in the last month. We used to get many people fleeing Bana, but that's rare now. They need new recruits."

Sorrel glanced around the barracks, counting twenty beds. "And how many of you?"

"In this barracks? Eight, counting your mother. But there's another barracks with closer to twenty. They keep us apart as much as they can."

"What else can you tell me?"

Petal shrugged. "Colonel Drax has a younger brother, Ganan. Drax blinded him with a torch. Made us all watch. Did it himself. Ganan hates him. Some of the younger Toplanders think Ganan should be colonel."

"A blind man?"

"They want the family to stay in control."

"Why hasn't someone killed this Drax?"

"You'd be surprised how well terror works to keep people from fighting back."

"What kind of weapons do they have?"

"Some guns. I don't know their names. One kind shoots hundreds of tiny pellets – they used to kill birds with it, until they realised ammunition was running out. Another kind fires a single shot and can kill someone far away. They carry the guns, but they hardly use them." Petal put her craft to one side and met Sorrel's eyes. "Why are you really here?"

"I told you the truth. But there's a group of Lowlanders, Tribals, I guess you'd call them, males and females, preparing to attack the camp. I want you all to help us. And I wanted to warn my mother. I don't want her to be killed in the fighting. Now I have to get her away from this Drax myself. I can't bear –".

"You? Alone? With a machete and a knife? Not a chance."

Silence fell. All the women were now sitting up, listening. Some left their beds and walked over.

"Where's the place where Drax does his – his – punishing?" Sorrel asked.

"One of the buildings. Half underground. We think it used to be an arms store, but there's a newer one where they keep weapons and ammunition now," Selan said. "It's cool in the day and soundproof. To the west of the old parade ground, close to the wall. But there are at least two guards when he's in there; sometimes three."

"I came over the wall near there. I only saw one guard on the wall."

"The door is on the north side. Tell us more about these people who are going to attack. What're they hoping to do?"

"We're all starving. There's water and food here and it can be defended. We could be in charge. Don't you see? This is our best chance. If we get rid of Colonel Drax, the Toplanders will be leaderless. If you help us, I can go back, warn my friends, stop them from attacking everyone and together we can get rid of this terrible man."

"When are they coming, these Tribals?" Petal asked. "How many of them?"

"Forty. Tonight."

"Huh. About the same number as the Toplanders," Selan said. "But we're locked in."

"Is there another way out of here? Do these windows open?"

"They're nailed shut. We've tried."

"Do you have tools?"

"No."

"I have a knife and a machete."

"You know what'll happen to you if they catch you?" the woman with the round face said.

"I don't want to know," Sorrel replied. "You're Iris?"

She nodded. "The dust might clear anytime."

"We brought a PlAK from Bana. The dust will get thicker. It'll be with us for at least two days, maybe more." She looked at each woman in turn. "Will you help us? We don't have time for all this talk."

175

"Here's what I can tell you," Selan said. "Don't try to leave the way you came in. There's an open drain not far from this building. That direction." She pointed. "It goes under the outside wall."

"Why haven't you used it?"

Selan sighed. "The girl who found it – they caught her a week later. Her name was Logan. She wasn't here long, used to wander off when we were in the gardens. Scouting, she called it. She told us about the drain. Some of us wanted to try, others thought that surviving outside was far worse than being here. She left one night, and LT caught her. They made us watch what they did to her and it took two days. After that, nobody wanted to even look for the drain."

"I might get lost."

"You have a machete. You can bushwhack. Just follow the wall to the gully. It's steep and treacherous, but you'll make it. After you come out of the drain, turn south." More of the females came closer, their faces grave.

"I don't think those high windows are nailed tight," Selan said. "They're for ventilation. The slats might come out."

"How would we get up there? We'd need to put the slats back after, or we'll all be punished."

The women stared up at two high triangular windows, at opposite ends of the barracks. "We don't know this stranger," Iris said, nodding at Sorrel. "Why are we risking anything for her? I don't want another beating. The last one nearly killed me." One of her eyes was half closed and she had a wide scar through an eyebrow.

"It's a risk for her too, Iris," Selan said.

"If we leaned up one of the bed frames, I think we could get up there," Petal said. "Let's at least try. If we have to destroy the slats to take them out, then –."

"Give me your knife," Petal said to Sorrel. "Iris, Selan, Odessa, take the bedding and let's lean up the frame."

The bed made a rickety ladder, but the women held it steady. Petal climbed up and ran her fingers around the small window. "I think the whole thing can come out, and then we can just put it back after," she said. "I'm not sure she can get through it, though."

176

"How will we hold it in place?"

"Just screw it back."

Sorrel sat on the bed and waited. If she left now to warn Arc, Caroni and the others, she would be leaving Bibi with Colonel Drax that much longer. Indecision tore at her. In her mind, she heard her mother saying: *Make a plan, One.*

Petal leaned against the window, using Sorrel's knife to turn the screws. It was slow, painstaking work and the knife kept slipping. She pocketed each screw as it came free. "Last one," she grunted, and then handed the triangular window down to Iris. "Measure the frame against your shoulders," Petal said to Sorrel, climbing down. "If you can get them through, you'll get the rest of your body out. Hurry now."

"I'll manage," Sorrel said. "Do you have any grease?"

"No grease."

Sorrel stood up and approached the upright bed.

She put her feet on the frame. "You don't have any weapons, right?

"No," Selan said.

"Keep my knife." She passed it over to Petal. "Do you think you could take this bed apart? It feels like it's been screwed together. Maybe you'll need the pieces."

"For what?" Selan said.

"To fight."

Sorrel climbed up to the vent and began squeezing her body through it.

CHAPTER 34 – COLONEL DRAX

The dust was even thicker outside, the sky a dirty orange. Sorrel dropped to her hands and knees and began to crawl in the direction Selan had indicated. She felt the shape of flat stones under her palms and hoped that following them would take her to the drainage system. Her hands found a low circular ridge which she realised was the edge of the drain. It was a shallow cylinder, easily able to hold her body. It disappeared down the steep hill.

She slid down it, feet first, scraping her limbs and tearing her clothes, her breathing ragged. The drain became steeper and smoother as she slid down it, barely able to control her descent.

She fell heavily at the end and for a moment felt disoriented and lost. *Follow the wall*, Selan had said. She untied her machete and swung it at the heavy bush, but the exertion made her feel faint. She leaned against the stones, drawing deep breaths. After a while her breathing calmed and she straightened up. Judging from the heat, it was mid-afternoon. She looked up and just above her head, saw the high wall encircling Cibao. Following it, she fought her way through the bush in what she hoped was the direction of the gully. She lost her footing several times and slid further down the steep slope. She couldn't see what was beneath her and knew it could be a sheer drop. She came to a loose pile of debris, probably deposited by an earthquake, which barred her way. *I can't*, she thought. Her vision darkened and her last thought was to protect her head as she fell.

Someone slapped her cheek and she opened her eyes. Rapt's face was above her – too close. "What the *guata* are you doing?" he said in his gravel voice. "Why'd you leave us? We had to waste time searching for you. Were you in the camp? Did you warn them?"

"No, of course not." Her voice raked at her throat. "Do you have water? Where are the others? What time is it?"

Rapt handed her his algaskin. "Get up," he said. "We're over there behind that pile of rubble. I heard when you fell – so I came to look. It's nearly dusk."

"Take me to Caroni. And Arc."

The Tribals sat in groups in the gully at the base of the collapsing wall. Emrallie got up. "Sorrel," she said. "*Guata*. Why'd you leave us?"

"I wanted to –" She stopped.

"Give her some room," Caroni said and Emrallie stepped back. "And keep your voices down." She turned to Sorrel. "Now talk." Sorrel heard the mistrust in the Zorah's voice.

"I wanted to warn my mother. Thought maybe I could bring her back and leave her in the valley. But then I wondered if the Lowlanders would join us. That would improve our chances."

"She talked to me about it," Rapt said. "She asked if inside help would work. I told her it was a good idea."

"Why didn't you just tell me?" Caroni said. "It's a decent plan – not the part about rescuing your mother but – "

"I knew that once I said Bibi's name you wouldn't listen." She looked around at the others and met Emrallie's eyes. "Nobody would've listened. You'd have tried to talk me out of trying."

"Why're you here without your mother, then?" Arc said, standing beside Caroni.

"Colonel Drax has her in his torture room – that's what the women told me. I figured getting help would be easier."

"Go on," Caroni said.

She told them what she'd learned – the numbers, the Lowlander women locked in from the outside, the second cabin of women she'd not seen, the basic layout of the camp, including the parade ground, the patrols, the drain she'd used to escape, and the sunken building near the south wall, where Colonel Drax held her mother.

"You said this Colonel has your mother? What do you mean?" Caroni said.

Sorrel looked up at the Zorah. "He tortures them. Chooses one every month. Takes them into that building and hurts them.

179

Cuts them. Blinds them. Some have awful scars. He even blinded his own brother. They're afraid of him but I think some of them will join us. Some think the brother – Ganan – would make a better leader. We have to go now, Caroni. The dust is bad, but not as bad as it's going to get."

"We don't know anything about this brother and we can't trust *Toplanders*," Rashelope said.

"It's not a bad idea to get rid of a leader," Arc countered.

"Stealth is easier than outright attack," Rapt said, surprising everyone. 'Do you know where this brother is?"

"No," Sorrel said.

"Pity," Arc said. "We could split up. Some of us make the attack on Drax. Others find Ganan."

"Why?" Emrallie asked.

"To give him a choice," Arc replied. "If the Northerners are coming, we need as many people as we can get."

"We need to go," Rashelope said.

"Wait," Sorrel said. "Half of us can climb up the drain I came down in – I'm sure Emrallie can do it and then set ropes from above for everyone else. She can find the Lowlanders and let them out – there's a bolt on the outside of their cabin door. They'll tell where Ganan is. The rest of us will approach from this side and find Drax."

"Won't the other guards hear us?"

"Remember the map I drew? Cibao is on a hill and the wall is below. The land falls away steeply on the northern side and there aren't many guards over there. I don't think they would be able to hear. Plus the dust helps us."

"We'd have to use knives and machetes," Rapt said. "Not guns. They could have communication equipment – radios or old-time walkie-talkies."

"Everything has a risk," Rashelope said.

"Anything else you want to tell us, Sorrel?" Caroni said.

"Just that we have to go soon."

"Wait here, people," Caroni said. "Arc, let's talk."

Arc and Caroni moved out of earshot and spoke in low voices. Sorrel met Rapt's eyes in the gloom and wanted to thank him, but said nothing. They waited.

"D'you know how long it took you?" Arc said, returning. "To get from there to here?"

Sorrel shook her head. "Just follow the wall and keep looking up for the drain."

"I think it's a crazy plan," Rashelope said.

"Me too," Emrallie said. "I'd rather die than be captured."

"It's better if we're separated," Arc said. "One group of us could survive, even if the other…"

"Alright," Caroni cut in. "We're going to split up. Arc, you and your group find Drax. Take the best fighters. I'll find the Lowlander women. Sorrel, Emrallie, you come with me."

"I want to go with Arc," Rashelope said.

"Me too," Emrallie said.

"We need you to climb, Emrallie," Caroni said. "Don't argue. This is how it's going to be."

"My mother is there," Sorrel said. "I want to join Arc and his group."

"No," Caroni said. "You know where to find the – aah – slaves. You know where the drain is. You and Emrallie are coming with me. No more discussion. Where's a good place to gather after, Sorrel?"

"The parade ground. Can't miss it."

"Let's make this fast," Caroni said.

"I want the best fighters with me." Arc pointed at members of his band and they walked over to stand beside him. "Rashelope, that includes you."

"I-I'll come with you," Lichen said, and stepped forward.

"No, Lichen," Caroni said.

"I can fit into tiny places. Many of you can't."

Arc shrugged and looked at Caroni. She gestured in agreement.

Rapt went to stand beside Arc. "Drax and the guards," he said, looking straight at Sorrel. "They're ferals. That's all."

CHAPTER 35 – GANAN

It was fully dark by the time the group led by the Zorah got to the drain. All the males had gone with Arc's group.

"We should risk using the PlAK's light," Sorrel whispered to Caroni. "The dust is really thick, and it might save us a lot of time – we don't want to just blunder past the drain." She burned with adrenaline and was glad Emrallie was with them on this night.

"I see something above," Genus muttered. "I think it's the end of the drain. Look up there."

It seemed too soon, but in the PlAK's dim light, they all saw it.

"Your turn, Emrallie," Caroni said.

Sorrel stood beside her friend and risked shining the search-light up the drain. "It's short," Emrallie said, looking up. "I'll climb up beside it, using the rocks. Can you keep the light on?"

"Go as fast as you can," Caroni said. Emrallie rubbed dirt on her gloves and jumped for a handhold that Sorrel couldn't see. They waited, struggling to breathe in the dust, watching Emrallie climb.

A rope snaked down. "Come up one at a time," Emrallie whisper-shouted from above.

Sorrel stowed away the PlAK and grasped the rope. She held her body away from the drain as Emrallie had once shown her in Jiba. "Anchor your feet," she'd explained. "Climbing's for legs, not arms. And keep looking up."

They stood at the edge of the camp, just inside the wall. "There's the cabin where the women sleep," Sorrel whispered, pointing to the outline of the building just ahead.

"We can hardly see anything," Caroni said. "Are you sure you can find your way across the camp?"

"The women can. Or we can use the PlAK, if we go quickly."

"They're locked in, you said? With a key?"

"Sounded like bolts; I'm not sure."

"Let's look. You lead, Sorrel. Everyone else, wait here."

The cabin door was held closed with deadbolts on the outside. There was a lock, but it was old. Caroni eased the bolts back and they squeaked.

"LT?" said a voice from inside. "Did you bring the soup?"

"It's me," Sorrel said. "Me and others. Let us in."

"I'll get the rest," Caroni said, as the door opened.

"Leave one person outside," Sorrel said.

"Why?"

"They can pull the bolts after we go in. If the guard comes back, he'll think everything is as he left it. Hurry."

Tribals and Lowlanders gathered inside the barracks. It was dark and stuffy; an old-time flashlight on the wall gave some light.

"Our water's nearly done," Selan said. "What's happening?"

"This is our Zorah, Caroni," Sorrel said, looking around at the women. Some stood close; others sat on beds, watching. Two women were under their bedding, faces turned away. "The males and some of our band are coming up the gully. Did you manage to make any weapons?"

"A few. We got three slats off one of the metal beds. Two of the table legs. Plus your knife."

"Are you with us?" Sorrel said.

"I'm coming," Selan said, fingering the scar on her cheek.

"I'm with you," Petal said.

"Not me," Hazel said. "You're all crazy."

The two on beds didn't stir.

"We know a path that hardly anyone uses on the other side of the vegetable garden. It's a little longer, but it'll take us right to Ganan's front door," Iris said.

"What about the women in the other cabin? Is it worth trying to get them to join us?"

Selan shook her head. "No time for persuading."

Caroni nodded.

Nine women crept across the camp, rudimentary weapons in their hands. "Stay on the path," Selan whispered. Emrallie was in front of Sorrel, who resisted the urge to touch her friend's shoulder as she had done on so many other journeys. Dust settled on their faces and shoulders. Their footsteps on the gravel path sounded too loud.

"This is Ganan's cabin," Selan said. They were outside one of the houses with a peaked roof.

"Will he open the door for you?" Caroni asked.

"Maybe."

"When he opens the door, we rush him," Emrallie said.

"Doesn't he have a guard?" Sorrel asked.

"For what? He's blind, we're locked in and the guards are on the wall. Ganan's not expecting an enemy in the camp."

Selan knocked on the door.

"He's not going to hear that," Sorrel said.

"He's blind. He relies on his hearing."

A male voice answered. "Who's there?"

"Sir. It's Selan. From the barracks. One of us is very sick, bleeding."

"You're supposed to be locked in! How'd you get out?"

"I guess LT forgot. Please, sir. We know you have medical supplies. We think it's that new bleeding fever."

The door opened and a dark-skinned man stood there. He wore dark glasses and stared upwards, his head cocked to one side. He looked about Bibi's age, with receding hair and a heavy brow. Selan ran up the steps and shoved him hard. He stumbled and fell, and the women rushed into his cabin, closing the door behind them.

There was an old-time lamp on a table attached to a battery pack, but the lamp was off. Caroni turned it on. Ganan sat on the floor, his hands outstretched. "You'll die for this," he said. "Whoever you are."

Sorrel stepped forward and held her machete at the side of his neck. "My name is Sorrel," she said. "I come from Bana. I'm here with dozens of Lowlanders and Tribals. We're all armed, and I'll cut your throat as easily as I would a porc. More easily. Your brother has hurt these women and he has my mother now."

"What do you want?"

"I'm the leader of the Tribals," Caroni said, bringing her face right up to the face of the blind man. "You have a choice here. You need us. Northerners are coming. On big ships. They will want this camp."

Ganan laughed. "You'll have to do better than that, woman."

"Why would we lie?"

"A dozen reasons. Okay, I'll bite. How do you know of this invasion?"

"We saw the ships. On our PlAK. Sorrel – the one with the machete at your neck – hacked into Level 1."

Ganan said nothing.

"Just *guatan* kill him," Emrallie said. "He's a Toplander."

"Yes, kill him," Selan said.

"Wait." Ganan pushed his glasses up onto his head. His eye sockets were livid holes with no lids and his whole face was scarred. Sorrel looked away and took the machete away from his neck.

"Tell me the whole story," he said.

Then they heard a shot.

"*Guata*," Sorrel said.

CHAPTER 36 – CONFLICT

They left Petal and Iris with Ganan. "Tie his hands and feet," Caroni ordered, throwing her a length of rope. Then they ran towards the sound of the shot, Emrallie in front. Sorrel's lungs felt as if they were full of mud. She expected the Toplanders to pour out of their buildings and overpower them at any time. She heard the clang of metal against metal and a low, bubbling cry just ahead, but the dust was too heavy to see clearly. She thought she heard Kes's voice.

"There it is," Selan panted. "Right there!"

Dim shapes became visible at the door of the half-buried building. Three Toplander guards stood in a semicircle with their backs to the door. Two had their hands raised. One was bringing his rifle to his shoulder when Rashelope erupted and with one swift swing of her machete, she split his head. He fell without a word. Rapt knelt, aiming the gun that Sorrel knew was empty at the other two guards. Kes picked up the guns that the surrendering guards had dropped. Sorrel pushed them aside and tried the door, but it was locked. "Tell the Colonel to come out," she said to Selan, who was beside her. "Tell him we're here, and more are coming."

"It needs to be the voice of a man. If he hears women, he'll know something is wrong."

Sorrel looked around. Rashelope was standing over the dead guard, bloody machete in her hand. Another guard lay face down, hands behind his head, his chest heaving. Rapt stood behind the third with his gun between the man's shoulder blades. The guard's face was scarred and his mouth was bracketed with the lines of age. Sorrel wondered if Drax spent his cruelty on his own people as well.

186

"Speak to your Colonel," Rapt growled and prodded the guard with the gun. "Do it, or I'll shoot you through the hips and you'll never walk, *guata* or piss again without help."

The guard lifted his head and shouted, "Colonel! You need to come out now. The camp is under attack!"

"Who's that?"

"I'm Mitchell. Corporal Mitchell."

"Where's Lieutenant Shan?"

"D-dead," said the guard. "Shan is dead, and Sherlock is captured. You need to come out. Please, Sir. Now. We need the key to the armoury."

As soon as the door swung open, Sorrel ran at the man with her machete upraised. They collided and fell. She smelled shit and caught a fleeting glimpse of a figure chained to the wall by one hand. She leapt to her feet and saw a bald man, thickset, dressed in camouflage, reaching for a handgun on a desk behind him. She swung the machete at his head with all her force. The blow connected just above his ear. He put his hand to his cheek, as if trying to hold his head straight. Then he dropped to his knees and rolled over onto the wet, black floor.

She looked up and saw Rapt standing in the room. "You're a warrior," he said, nodding. "I never..." He kicked at the man on the floor.

"Where are the others?" she gasped.

"Fighting. See to your mother." He turned on his heel and left. She shut and locked the door and walked over to the crumpled figure against the wall, grateful for the soft light in the room.

"Bibi?" she said, kneeling.

There was no response and Sorrel's body went cold. She cupped her mother's chin and gently lifted her face. Bibi's eyes were unfocused, but she felt her mother's halting breath on her hand. Her cheek was bleeding. "Bibi?" she said again.

Bibi stirred, her eyes fluttered open. "One? Is it really you?"

"It's me. How badly are you hurt? Can you stand? Where's the key for that shackle?"

"Left hand drawer, the table behind you," Bibi whispered.

Sorrel unlocked the chain and tried to guide Bibi to a narrow bed in the middle of the room.

"No," she said. "I won't lie there. There's drinking water on the table – bring that to me. I'll be fine on the floor. Drag that – that man out of here. Then go, One. Do what you have to do. Shut the door when you leave but don't lock it."

"I'll send one of the women," Sorrel said. She leaned down, grabbed Drax by his boots and dragged him out the door.

Outside, there were no more sounds of fighting and the dust was a solid thing around her. She ran in the direction of the gully. Arriving at the wall, she saw several figures standing in a circle, looking down. Rapt was there, gun over his shoulder. Caroni and Emrallie were supporting each other. Rashelope had her machete in one hand and her shovel in the other. Kes stood inside the circle, a small pile of clothing at his feet. The camp women who had joined the fight stood around in silence.

Sorrel walked up to Kes. Tears had drawn lines through the dust on his face.

"What happened?" she said. "Where are the other guards?" She reached out to touch him, and he stepped back, stumbling a little.

"It's Lichen," Rashelope said. "Someone shot her. In the back. Maybe it was one of us."

"Was that the shot I heard?" Sorrel stammered.

"Does it matter?" Rashelope said.

"It doesn't," Caroni said.

Lichen lay face down in the dirt. "Don't touch her. I don't want to see her face," Emrallie said, her voice choked.

"Was anyone else hurt?" Sorrel said.

"Journey is dead. Also another of yours – aah – Genus, I think her name is – was," Kes said. "Some of us are hurt, yes. Slate lost a hand. I don't think Sandstorm will make it."

"Where are the wall guards?"

"Dead. They weren't young and didn't expect anyone from the inside. We pushed them over the wall. Did you find Ganan?"

"Yes. Two of the camp women are holding him. What about the other guards? The ones on the other side? They must have heard the shot."

"I don't know. Arc led some of our band to find them and they haven't come back."

188

Caroni lifted her head. "Go and look for them, Kes. Take at least six of your band – I think there are three or four guards unaccounted for." She looked down at Lichen's crumpled figure. "Kill them, if they don't surrender. Do you have string or rope? If they give up their weapons, tie them up where you find them. How bad is your shoulder?"

"It can wait. See to Slate and Sandstorm. They're over there, and I think they're badly hurt."

Caroni faced the others, but before she could speak again, Rashelope leaned down to lift Lichen's lifeless body. Her shoulders shook and Sorrel knew she was crying although she could not see her face. She felt a breath of wind and looked up – perhaps the dust would lift at last. She heard footsteps behind her and turned.

Petal and Iris led Ganan towards them, his face raised to the sky.

Caroni stopped in front of him, placing her hand flat on his chest. He spoke before she could say anything. "Is my brother dead?"

"He is."

"Good. What about others?"

"Others are dead too."

"I meant our people."

"I know what you meant. You need us. We can help. There's worse coming."

Ganan was silent. More people were arriving out of the gloom, the Lowland women who had been enslaved, Arc behind four Toplander guards – all with their hands raised.

"Who are your leaders?" Ganan said.

"I am," Arc said, stepping forward. "I'm Arc."

"I'm Caroni."

"My name is Ganan – Drax's brother."

"We know."

"There's an old cemetery here," Ganan said. "We'll bury our fallen tomorrow at dawn. Then, we'll eat and talk. Lieutenant Faldo!"

"Sir!" said one of the Toplander men with his hands up.

"Stand everybody down. Let the women in Barracks C out."

The Tribals climbed up to the parade ground in the dark, some nursing injuries, holding arms and shoulders, limping, staunching wounds with rags. Stretchers had been found for Slate and Sandstorm. Rashelope still cradled Lichen's body, her face lowered to the dead girl's and Kes carried Genus's body in his arms. The Toplanders slung the dead guards over their shoulders and plodded uphill. Colonel Drax was left on the step outside the half-buried building. The wind blew more strongly and stirred the dust around them. Sorrel looked up, searching for the prick of stars, but the dust still covered them all.

"We'll have to wait for morning to sort things out," Caroni said to Ganan. "Which is the biggest room?"

"'A' barracks," he said.

"Send someone to bring all the Toplanders to the barracks," Caroni said. "Everyone must stay together tonight. Go with him, Kes."

"Selan, is it?" Caroni said. "Go and brief the women in the other cabin. Tell them to stay inside until morning. You wait there with them."

"I'm going to get my mother," Sorrel said.

"I'll come with you," Emrallie said.

Bibi sat in a corner of the half-buried room, her head held back, eyes closed. Sorrel bent down and held her, feeling her body shake. Bibi's hair was almost shoulder length and her arms were taut with muscle. Sorrel wiped her mother's cheek – the cut was ragged.

"What did he do to you?"

"It's not important. Nothing permanent. This bite on my face might get infected. That's about the worst of it."

"Can you walk?"

"I think so." Bibi looked up. "Emrallie, right?"

"Yes. Take my hand," Emrallie said.

"I remember you. You saved my daughter's life when she fell into that pool. Is the fighting over?"

"For now," Emrallie said.

In the large barracks, the injured were laid on the lower bunk beds. Others claimed the remaining beds or sat on the floor in small groups. Four of the Toplanders were trembling, grey-haired old men; they lowered themselves slowly to one of the beds, not speaking, but clinging to each other. Two carried walking sticks, objects from another time, another civilization, with metal handles and carved shafts. The other Toplanders streamed in, men and women, some in night clothes Sorrel had only ever seen on the internet. Few were young. She began counting as they filed in and stopped at twenty-nine – more women than men. It was hard to believe that so few people had controlled the camp and terrorized a city.

The wind was rising. Several of the enslaved camp women stood guard against the walls, disbelief carved on their faces.

Sorrel sat with Bibi on one of the beds and they told their stories to each other in low voices. "Northerners are coming," she told her mother. "The satellites are being disabled."

Bibi nodded. "They'll want the water here." She shifted her position and groaned.

"What do you need? What can I do for you?"

"Nothing, One. Time is all I need." She paused. "Did you find what you were looking for; with the Tribals, I mean?"

"Yes, I guess so," she said. "But I wanted you to be there too. I mourned you, Mom. I mourned you." The unfamiliar name hovered between them.

"I know, One. I know. I wanted to spare you."

"I saw your message," she said.

Bibi touched her face. "I had to hope you would be fine with the Tribals."

Iris walked over to them. "I'm going to the kitchen. I think we all need food. Hazel says there are a lot of eggs. And at least six breadfruit for frying."

"You have *eggs*?" Sorrel said.

"We re-domesticated some avians."

"Do you think it can work?" Sorrel asked her mother, after Iris had left. "Toplanders and Lowlanders? Males and females living together?"

"A lot of things once seemed impossible," said Bibi. "No one thought we could get the avians to lay eggs in cages. But we did.

Lowlanders can't imagine a place with old-time rain. We have it here."

"Or berries and breadfruit," Sorrel added.

"Or a world without satellites."

Sorrel's eyelids felt heavy. Her exhaustion was bone deep, but she was grateful not to be injured. She stretched out on the bed beside Bibi and thought of Lichen's courage and Genus's death and Slate's severed hand and the abdominal wound that would probably kill Sandstorm. She wondered if any of the Toplanders were healers. Then she thought about the eggs she would soon eat, and her stomach roiled. She felt calm, as at the end of something. She looked over at Emrallie and Rashelope and Rapt, standing guard at one end of the barracks and then at the shapes of the Toplanders, huddled around Ganan's bed. It felt safe enough to sleep.

She dreamed of the rock she had hidden underneath in childhood and the blistering of her cheek, and in her sleep, she thought she felt her mother's palm against her face. She dreamed of standing at the waterfall with Kes, the sweat on her skin becoming the mist of the waterfall and Rapt watching them with tears running down his cheeks.

An earth tremor rippled through the camp, but no one reacted. Sorrel slept. It was night.

She woke when dawn glimmered through the shutters. She sat up, gasping at the stiffness in her limbs and the pain of bruises she could not remember getting. Bibi still slept beside her; the bite made by Drax's teeth livid on her cheek. A calabash hung from a hook on the wall next to the bed. Petal's work. She took it down. It held two boiled eggs and a piece of fried breadfruit.

She took the food and her algaskin and tiptoed to the door. Outside, the dust had cleared, and pale grey clouds tinged with the pink of sunrise gathered, threatening rain. She looked over the patches of growing crops, most of which she didn't recognize. She wondered where the river was. *Homeplace,* she thought. Somewhere worth defending.

She walked along the path she'd travelled the previous night, until she came to the parade ground. She pulled her dark glasses from her pocket, thinking of Ganan's sightless eyes, but they dimmed her vision too much and she pushed them onto her head. She walked past the building where her mother had been tortured; Drax's body was still on the steps and she heard the buzzing of flies. This morning, Lichen and Genus and Journey, and Toplanders whose names she did not yet know, would be buried in an old cemetery along with the stories of uncounted others from decades and centuries past. She went to the edge of the broken concrete area and looked out, wanting to see the island clearly, for what it was, for what it had become – stripped of forests, blasted by hurricanes, burned by fires, riven by earthquakes, chewed at by landslides. But still – the mountains stood. At the very limit of her vision, she could see the darker blue of the empty sea, all the way to a blurred horizon, which would bring the Northerners, perhaps to Cibao itself, and they would have to fight to hold onto the camp. Would there be many more acts of violence she would have to commit? She thought of the story of her father swinging an axe at the skynut tree and her own blow to Drax's head

"What're you doing?" Emrallie said from behind her. "Why've you taken off your glasses?"

"Just wanted to see clearly. For a few seconds." They stood together, looking south, to the sea.

"Do you think we can beat the Northerners?" Sorrel said.

"All depends on what tech they have. Not if they have military drones. Maybe in hand-to-hand combat. We have the advantage of knowing the place and holding the higher ground, but…"

"Maybe they won't come here at all."

"If the PlAK fails, will we be able to see them coming?" Emrallie asked, staring out to sea.

"Yes, from here. If there's no dust or hurricane or wildfire, we'll see them coming."

The settled dust whirled away, zephyrs of wind made visible. Sorrel replaced her dark glasses and stared at the battered island below. *Darkest before dawn*, she thought. And here, there was dawn with less danger. For now.

She reached into the calabash she carried. "Want an egg?"

"You have it. I had enough last night."

"D'you think we'll be okay up here, Em? Living with males, maybe women getting pregnant? Jealousies? Babies?

"*Guata*, Sorrel! Just eat the egg." Then Emrallie smiled.

AUTHOR'S NOTE

This book had its genesis in a 2017 internet story about the impact of extreme heat on those who lived or worked outdoors in India – mainly construction workers, farmers, or people without adequate shelter. I started thinking about what it would mean for a tropical country, like my own, if it became too dangerous to be outside in the day, for at least some portion of the year. What occupations would be affected? Would we still be able to grow food? What would happen if roads melted? Suppose it got so hot that we all had to work at night and sleep in the day? And suppose there was a girl, a teenager, who simply couldn't sleep during the day?

In the two years since I began writing *Daylight Come*, I've seen much that I imagined in a hot new world actually occurring – fires, floods, droughts, crop failures, heat waves, desperate people on the move. The climate crisis is here and now, but worse is ahead, if we do not change course.

Given that I've spent almost three decades as an environmental activist, young people often ask me, what is to be done? We have to tell stories, I reply. Engage people's imaginations. Their emotions, their connections to home and family. To place. My hope for *Daylight Come* is that it will do just that.

The place names in the Caribbean came from Taino words and I used the old names for continents and oceans. We humans so often rename the places we encounter, in part to hide our crimes against each other and against nature, so I wanted the climate catastrophe to trigger just such a reinvention. A discerning reader will see the Jamaican bones which underlie the island of Bajacu in 2084, but I've not been constrained by actual geography and *Daylight Come* is a work of fiction.

Thanks to my first and always generous readers – Freddy, Celia, Esther, Jonathan, Polly and Yasmin. I'm grateful for the BURT Prize for Caribbean Literature, which awarded a third place prize to an earlier version of *Daylight Come*. Thanks to all at Peepal Tree Press – Jeremy Poynting and Hannah Bannister, and especially to Jacob Ross, whose keen editorial attention made *Daylight Come* a much better book.

Here's hoping this book remains forever in the category of speculative fiction.

ABOUT THE AUTHOR

Diana McCaulay is a Jamaican writer and environmental activist. She has written two novels, *Dog-Heart* (March 2010) and *Huracan* (July 2012), published by PeepalTree Press. Both novels met with critical acclaim and have broken local publishing records.

She has lived her entire life in Kingston, Jamaica and engaged in a range of occupations – secretary, insurance executive, racetrack steward, mid-life student, social commentator, environmental advocate. She is the founder and Board Chair of the Jamaican Environment Trust. She is also the recipient of the 2005 Euan P. McFarlane Award for Outstanding Environmental Leadership, a Bronze Musgrave Medal from the Institute of Jamaica, and National Honours, the Order of Distinction (Officer Class), for her environmental work.

Dog-Heart won a Gold Medal in the Jamaica Cultural Development Commission's National Creative Writing Awards (2008), was shortlisted for the Guyana Prize (2011), the IMPAC Dublin Award (2012) and the Saroyan Prize for International Writing (2012). *Huracan* was also shortlisted for the Saroyan Prize 2014.

ALSO BY DIANA McCAULAY

Dog-Heart
ISBN 9781845231231; pp. 244; pub. 2010; £9.99

Dog-Heart is a novel about the well-meaning attempt of a middle-class single mother to transform the life of a boy from the ghetto whom she meets on the street.

Set in present-day, urban Jamaica, *Dog-Heart* tells the story from two alternating points of view – those of the woman and the boy. They speak in the two languages of Jamaica that sometimes overlap, sometimes display their different origins and world views. Whilst engaging the reader in a tense and absorbing narrative, the novel deals seriously with issues of race and class, the complexity of relationships between people of very different backgrounds, and the difficulties faced by individuals seeking to bring about social change by their own actions.

Huracan
ISBN: 9781845231965; pp. 294; pub. 2012; £10.99

Back in Jamaica after years away, Leigh McCaulay encounters the familiarity of home along with the strangeness of being white in a black country, and struggles with guilt and confusion over her part in an oppressive history of white slave owners and black slaves.

As Leigh begins to make an adult life on the island, she learns of her ancestors – Zachary Macaulay, a Scot sent as a young man to be a bookkeeper on a sugar plantation in 18th century Jamaica who, after witnessing and participating in the brutality of slavery, becomes an abolitionist; and John Macaulay, a missionary who comes to Jamaica in the 19th century to save souls and ends up questioning the foundations of his beliefs.

Part historical and part contemporary literary fiction, loosely based on the author's own family history, *Huracan* explores how we navigate the inequalities and privileges we are born to and the possibilities for connectedness and social transformation in everyday contemporary life. But it is also the story of an island's independence; of the people who came (those who prospered and those who were murdered); of crimes and acts of mercy; and the search for place, love and redemption.